WILDFLOWERS:
AN END OF THE WORLD ROMANCE

NEW YORK TIMES BESTSELLING AUTHOR
KYLIE SCOTT

Proofreader: Lisa Wolff
Interior Book Design: Champagne Book Design
Cover Design: By Hang Le

ISBN: 978-0-6484574-3-5

END OF THE WORLD
RADIO STATION PLAYLIST

"It's the End of the World as We Know It (And I Feel Fine)"
by R.E.M.

"Death Don't Have No Mercy" by Rev. Gary Davis

"Thoroughfare" by Ethel Cain

"The End of the World" by Skeeter Davis

"If the World Was Ending" by JP Saxe, with Julia Michaels

"Wildflower" by Billie Eilish

"The Man Comes Around" by Johnny Cash

"Eve of Destruction" by Barry McGuire

"Wild Flower" by The Cult

"Five Years" by David Bowie

"Clarity" by Vance Joy

"99 Red Balloons" by Nena

"Funeral" by Phoebe Bridgers

"Don't Dream It's Over" by Crowded House

"1999" by Prince

"End of the World" by Miley Cyrus

"Bullet with Butterfly Wings" by The Smashing Pumpkins

"Wildflowers" by Tom Petty

WILDFLOWERS:

AN END OF THE WORLD ROMANCE

CHAPTER ONE

THURSDAY

"**G**OING SOMEWHERE?" ASKS A VOICE FROM OUT OF THE dark.

I clutch my market bag to my chest. "Shit!"

"Didn't mean to scare you."

The smile won't sit straight on my face. Not that he can see it behind my mask. You would think going grocery shopping at nine at night in old jeans and an even older tee would be safe. Of all the times for the dude from across the street to acknowledge my existence.

I'm average height and weight, with my long brown hair up in a messy bun. And there he stands at well over six foot something, shoulders as wide as Montana, dark hair showing traces of gray and giving me daddy issues, along with a jawline sharp enough to make a runway model weep. *Fuck.*

Which reminds me.

"You forgot your mask," I say.

"Sorry." He grimaces. "Promise I haven't had contact with anyone for days."

"Me neither."

"You haven't?"

"No. One of the many benefits of working remote."

Some tension in him eases at the news. Which is fair enough. "I didn't think you'd been out," he says. "But that's good to hear."

I lean my ample ass against my Prius and stare at him, bemused. Because what an odd thing to say. But most everyone is stuck at home now. He must be keeping an eye on the street out of boredom or something.

It's rare for our neighborhood in Portland, Oregon, to be so quiet. However, traffic tonight is nonexistent. Besides the ambulance speeding past with its siren wailing. The sound of someone coughing comes from the apartment building behind me. And the Thai restaurant on the corner is sadly closed. Probably due to staff shortages. Which sucks, because papaya salad would go a long way toward fixing what's wrong with me. That being having just about run out of food. But the combination of seasonal allergies and some new strain of flu have made a mess of the city this week.

Hot Neighbor constantly turns his head, glancing up and down the street. Just checking things out, apparently. He's much larger close up than I realized. Then he looks down at me, and I look up at him, and…yeah. This situation is giving me such a weird vibe. Though I do find beautiful people stressful to deal with in general.

And when I get nervous, I babble.

"The world is so discombobulated right now. Do you know, I tried to get groceries delivered but everywhere was booked out? I couldn't find a single place. Most of their workers must be off sick. I know the government said to stay home as much as possible. But I'm sure you would agree that when a woman runs out of cake, drastic action must be taken. Some odds are just insurmountable, right? A step beyond what's humanly possible to endure. Okay. I better go get this done before the shops close." I reach for the car door. "Nice to meet you."

"You didn't tell me your name."

"You didn't tell me yours."

He gives me this smile. The whole time we've been talking, he's had a hand behind his back. I don't even know why I notice, since it's just the way he's standing.

"Dean."

"Astrid."

"That's a pretty name."

"Thank you." I open the door. "See you later, Dean."

Guess I shouldn't have turned my back on him. But then, I didn't expect him to attack. Stupid me.

I catch movement out of the corner of my eye. His arms come swiftly around me from behind. My mask is pushed aside and something covers my mouth and nose. A cloth that's been doused in some chemical. It smells sort of sweet.

I scratch and kick as my mind spins in dizzy circles. But it all happens so fast, and the world goes dark.

FRIDAY

I wake up on a mattress on the floor. Nothing hurts. That's the main thing. And my clothes seem to be untouched; only my shoes and mask are missing.

The man sitting on the other side of the room says, "Drink some water. You'll feel better."

My mind is a mess. I don't know whether to be terrified, furious, or what. More information is needed.

On the mattress is a clean white sheet along with a pillow, a padded quilt, and a warm gray woolen blanket. And on the floor sits a worn Persian rug in shades of red. The walls are bare brick, the low ceiling wooden, and the only window I can see is high and narrow and covered in some sort of thick, dark padding. Which means shouting for help is probably a waste of time. This must be the bottom level of his bungalow. Which is reason enough to lose my shit in a variety of ways.

But add the fact that I am sitting inside a makeshift cage, a prison for all intents and purposes, and I can't stop my hands from shaking. Like actual solid metal bars cut across the space between us.

"What the fuck, Dean?"

He nods to the bottle of water waiting beside the bed.

I sit up slowly and reach for it. The seal seems to be intact. But what do I know?

"I haven't tampered with it," he says. "It's safe to drink."

Our staring competition lasts half a minute or so. Though conflict may not be the answer to this particular problem. My current position isn't exactly one of strength, what with me sitting in an enclosure. Seems spending all of those hours watching cute animal videos and contouring tutorials instead of learning negotiation tactics and tips and tricks from escape artists might have been a mistake.

I take the top off the bottle and sip cautiously. It doesn't taste any different than ordinary water. And I am indeed thirsty. "What did you drug me with?"

"Chloroform. Thought you'd only be out for a while, but you slept the whole night. Must have been tired."

Iron fencing divides the room down the middle. His side has a large TV, a plaid sofa, a punching bag, a bunch of storage boxes, and—most importantly—stairs leading up to the outside world and freedom. My side has a mattress and access to a small bathroom.

He's placed the bars horizontally. It must have been the best way for the sections of fencing to fill the space. Then he welded the panels together. And while it may not be pretty, it will keep me here just fine. One piece of the fence is held in place with thick lengths of chain and padlocks to work as a door.

I nod at the wall of iron. "I take it this used to be your back fence?"

"Yeah. The neighbors aren't happy." Shadows linger beneath his eyes and stubble lines his jaw. Seems the asshole needs a nap and a shave. "I want to make a deal with you."

"Do I have a choice?"

"No."

"Shitty deal. Why are you doing this?"

"It's complicated. But I'm not going to hurt you," he says. "You won't come to any harm while you're with me."

"Besides the harms of being abducted and imprisoned?"

"Yes."

The urge to scream and start throwing things is immense. But I take a breath and hold my shit together. Just. "You promise you won't touch me or make me do anything?"

"That's right. You have my word. But I *am* going to insist on the pleasure of your company for a while."

"Why?"

He picks up the remote and the TV comes to life. The news channel is running the same reports as yesterday. Photos of a crowded hospital in Beijing. Sick children in Cairo with mucus running down their faces. But it's the dead body lying out on the street in Brisbane and a mass grave in Prague that really get to me.

I swallow hard. "My mother thinks the pictures will turn out to be AI or something."

"What do you think?"

"Pretty sure Reuters doesn't print fake news, and that's where I first saw them. But it's not going to get that bad here. We've been forewarned. We have masks and stuff."

"Masks are great. But they only filter out particles bigger than fifteen microns. They won't touch this virus."

"Well, they're working on a vaccine."

"They are. But that sort of thing takes time."

"Time you don't think we have."

His jaw shifts. "No."

"I believe that we do. This is going to be just like the last pandemic. Fucking awful, but nothing like what you're talking about. You need to let me go, Dean. Please."

"I'm glad you have hope," he says. "But I'm sorry, Astrid. You're staying in that cage where I know you'll be safe."

"What do you care if I'm safe or not?"

"I just do."

"That makes no sense." My whole body starts to shake. Not

good. "Last night was the first time we'd talked. We're veritable strangers, and you built me a prison cell in your basement."

"You're welcome." His gaze narrows on me. "Just breathe, Astrid. It's going to be okay. No one's going to hurt you, I promise."

"You have to let me out of here. And what happens if you're wrong about the virus?"

"You go free, and I go to jail," he says matter-of-factly.

I can't help but scoff. Though it sounds like more of a choked sob than anything else. My want to scream and rage and cry at him struggles with the need to stay calm and be rational and try to talk my way out of this. Though I have a feeling I'm fighting a losing battle. There's so much fear and frustration inside of me. "Are you saying you'll open my cage door and then, what…just hand yourself over to the cops?"

He crosses his arms. Angry red lines are visible from where I scratched him last night. "I might try making it to the border. But yes, I will just open your cage door once I know you're going to be safe."

Deep, even breaths. Passing out in a panic isn't going to help. I need to choose my words with care and talk him into setting me free. Get him to see me as a person with my own wants and rights and needs. "How long do I have to stay here? When will you admit that you made a mistake?"

"You want a time frame?"

"Yes, please."

"I don't know," he says. "Say a fortnight to be safe."

"You want me to sit in this cage for two weeks?"

"Think about it. We're probably going to know what's going on a hell of a lot sooner. The first time anyone heard of this virus was through some vague reports from Europe and Asia on Saturday. But by Sunday, it was already here and circulating amongst the general population. Forget quarantine measures failing. We never even had a chance to implement them," he says in a clear, concise voice. "As for the incubation period—you have someone picking a friend up from the airport Sunday afternoon and dying early Monday morning. There were underlying conditions in that case…but still. Others have reported a couple of days between first experiencing symptoms and succumbing to the virus."

"I know all of this."

He nods. "Good. That's good. Let me tell you something you might *not* know. The survival rate is zero, the communicability rate is through the roof, and the current death toll is millions more than we're being told."

"Oh, come on. You don't think that all sounds a little paranoid? I know there are a lot of conflicting reports on social media. But how would they hide that kind of thing from us?"

"By shutting down the schools and telling us to stay home and stay safe," he says. "Finding cause to block the largest social media site for the spread of news and information wouldn't have hurt either. And this isn't exactly the first time the government has lied to us about something."

"Okay. Why are they doing it?"

"To avoid people panicking."

"Where are you getting your information from?"

"I spent some time in the Marines. Just long enough to get shipped out, blown up, and discharged," he says with a rueful smile.

"So you have cause to hate the government."

"Doesn't everybody these days?" he asks. "But the point is, I still have friends that are active in those circles. One of them has been working for a private firm. They've got her moving people around for the CDC and evacuating government officials from Washington. That sort of thing."

"Washington?" I cock my head. "But their figures are low. They're doing great with social distancing and hand washing."

"The inner-city hospitals are full and they're about to run out of body bags. Then they'll start running out of doctors and nurses. Washington has such a transient and social population. All of those important people, flying around the world and having meetings. And it hasn't even been a week since we first heard of this thing."

"I'm just supposed to take your word for this?"

He nods at the TV. "They're not going to be able to hide the truth for much longer. Not with things going the way they are…"

"I have another question." I sit up straight and take a deep breath. "Have you ever done anything like this before?"

"No. My worst crimes before this were some speeding tickets and a bar fight in Boulder, Colorado. Which I didn't start, by the way."

"And does your friend know what you're doing to me?"

"She does not."

"Why me, Dean?" My hand itches to slap him. Not that it would help a thing. "Why am I important to you?"

He doesn't answer for a moment. "I have clear line of sight to your apartment door from my living room window, and…"

"You've been watching me?"

His jaw shifts, but he doesn't say a word. What an asshole.

"For how long?"

"Guess it's been a while now," answers my stalker. "The thing is, your trip out last night would have killed you. I *had* to stop you. But I would have had to do something sooner rather than later. Couldn't risk someone knocking on your door for whatever reason. Or you rushing off to help a sick friend or family member who could be contagious."

I shake my head. There's no talking him out of this delusion, however. "Can I have my phone?"

"Let's talk about that later."

"How high exactly is the mortality rate? Do you even know or are you just guessing?"

He frowns. And I mean, he really puts his whole heart and soul into the furrows happening on his high forehead. Then eventually, he says, "My friend was working close protection for a top government epidemiologist the first few days when all of this started. They seemed to think we're looking at ninety-nine percent of the population. Anything around those levels is Armageddon."

My mouth opens, but nothing comes out. Not for a while. "You don't really believe that. Come on. I watch the History channel, and not even the bubonic plague did those sorts of numbers. Not even close."

He just watches me.

"Dean, this is so wrong. Please. You have to let me out."

He stands tall and stretches. The man is all hard, lean muscle. And he sure would look pretty with my hands wrapped around his thick neck. "I'm sorry, but I'm not going to do that. You may as well get comfortable."

And this is when I officially lose my shit. "Let me out of here, you motherfucking asshole! You kidnapping cunt! Open this fucking cage right now. How dare you drug me and lock me up in here, you deluded dickhead!"

But he doesn't even hang around to hear my rant. His face blanks and up the stairs he goes, leaving me to scream my abuse to no one.

CHAPTER TWO

FRIDAY

MY CAPTOR RETURNS AN HOUR OR SO AFTER I STOP yelling. Something that happens due to a sore throat and eventually running out of expletives. I sincerely hope he sat upstairs and listened. Because the one about his marked resemblance to a goat's genitals was honestly inspired.

The first full day of captivity is mostly pleasant, all things considered. Which is surprising. Breakfast is buttermilk pancakes. The man knows how to cook and makes a decent cup of coffee. Both important life skills. My silverware is a child's silicone spoon. The chances of me successfully stabbing him with it are low. It would take a serious effort along with his cooperation to gouge his heart out with this sucker. And my coffee was served in a cardboard takeout cup, with the pancakes on a paper plate. He's thought through this hostage situation. Nothing he's given me can be used against him as a weapon.

I am doing my best to stay calm. It's sort of working.

The bathroom is small, with modern white tiling. Just room enough for a shower, basin, cupboard, and toilet. An array of products have been left for me. There's even some decent skin care. Dean didn't cheap out on anything. Guess if you're expecting the world to end, there's no need to worry about credit card debt. No cameras in the bathroom that I can find, thank fuck. Cleaning my teeth, brushing my hair, and applying deodorant have me feeling at least half human.

This is the longest I've gone without my phone. No scrolling social media or internet shopping or anything. Life in a cage or prison cell is about as boring as you'd imagine. Especially if not much is happening. And while being kept in captivity is all sorts of messed up, he's not actually hurting me. The mattress and cushions are quite comfortable. Even the décor is nice. Though if I wind up dead and buried in his backyard, the joke will be on me for letting my guard down for even a second.

Someone must have noticed me missing by now. Surely. Dean might have the logistics of kidnapping me covered, but he can't control everything. I had an online meeting scheduled with my boss this morning. Work could have noticed my absence and called the relevant authorities. For all I know, detectives are on their way here right now. However, I highly doubt it. My boss, Kate, is related to someone in upper management. She's likely to have forgotten about the meeting and gone to breakfast with her boyfriend. Insert heavy sigh here.

From my way of thinking, the best chance of getting out from behind these bars is by making Dean think we're friends. Just because my social skills suck in real-life situations doesn't mean I can't fake it upon this occasion. It will be fine. I can absolutely do this.

"How about you give me my phone for five minutes," I ask.

"I don't think you understand the stakes here. If I lose my streak on Wordle, I'll never forgive you."

It earns me a short laugh. But my captor doesn't deign to reply.

"What happens if you trip on the stairs and fall and break your neck or something, and I'm left alone in this cage to die a slow and painful death of starvation because no one knows I'm down here, and years from now someone discovers our desiccated bodies?"

He looks at me over the rim of his cup of coffee.

I shrug. "It could happen."

"There's an email scheduled to go out each day alerting the local police and other assorted emergency services, and a couple of other places I thought might be useful, as to your whereabouts."

"You stop it from sending."

"That's right," he says.

"Are they looking for me yet?"

"No. Not that I've noticed. But with everything going on and so many people off sick, I'd be surprised if the police had time to knock on doors for a missing person right now. And you've also only been gone for fourteen hours."

"It feels longer than that."

He grunts in response. Like a Neanderthal.

The TV is on, though muted, with captioning along the bottom of the screen. As the day progresses, the tone of reports seems to be shifting. Things seem distinctly more dire. Like the government is losing control of the narrative. Now they show how hospitals are struggling to keep up. Morgues and funeral homes are overwhelmed by the sheer number of deceased. The woman from the World Health Organization pauses her speech on current recommendations for how best to keep yourself safe to have a coughing fit on air.

My parents must be so scared. Dean can't be right about the world ending. He just can't be. I refuse to believe we're on the brink of societal collapse and most everyone I have ever met is going to die this week, or is in the process of dying. The very thought is like worms in my brain.

"What do you normally do?" I pace back and forth. "When you're not seeing to the caging, feeding, and care of the modern woman?"

This time his grunt is one of mirth. I have amused him again. Go, me.

"I work as a contractor," he says. "What about you?"

"Online customer service. How old are you?"

"Forty-two." He finishes wrapping tape around his hands and starts hitting the speed bag. A move that shows the muscles in his arms. "You?"

"Thirty-three. Are you trying to impress me with the boxing display?"

"That depends. Are you impressed?"

"No."

He just smiles.

There's a small chance that by *friends* I actually meant *frenemies*. It would seem my acting skills are insufficient for anything else.

I wondered what was going on when he reappeared after breakfast having changed out of last night's abduction outfit (jeans and a tee) into a different tee, a pair of sweatpants, and some jogging shoes. Perchance he would go running, giving me time to make a daring escape. I would have somehow grown the strength to bend iron bars and liberate myself. Just gone Godzilla on the cage. It would have been so great.

I never did like zoos as a child. All of the watching wild animals pace back and forth behind the bars. Having now been on the receiving end of just such a situation, I can confirm it is complete and utter bullshit. Zero stars. Do not recommend. Big jungle cats mauling their keepers makes so much more sense to me now. I am surprised it doesn't happen more often.

"Did you grow up around here?" I ask, resting my arms on the bars.

"Yeah."

"I'm from San Francisco originally."

"You mentioned a mother." He holds to his rhythm, hitting the bag. His feet move almost as if he's dancing. "She still down there?"

"Both of my parents are, and my brother lives near them with his partner. We had Christmas together. It was nice."

The reporting on the TV changes to traffic jams and pile-ups. Seems people are trying to flee the cities to escape the virus. It's not a bad idea, but it's obviously not an original one. Every bridge and expressway exiting a city is now bumper-to-bumper.

"I don't have any family," he says without prompting. This must be the getting-to-know-you stage of things. He seems willing to open up when it comes to personal information, if not cage doors.

"Do you have many close friends?" I ask.

He just shrugs. Guess the personal information stage is over already. That was fast.

Someone's car alarm has been sounding off for about fifteen

minutes now. Bizarre how no one has done anything about it. This is generally a nice neighborhood. Helicopters also keep flying overhead. It would seem the skies are busy today.

My hands are shaking again. But I've found any time the bars start to press in on me, some nice deep, even breathing calms things down. Having a panic attack isn't going to help anything. Just hope I can keep it under control.

"There are people I talk to regularly and watch films with or go out to dinner or to a concert or whatever…but I'm okay just doing stuff on my own," I say. "I guess I've always spent time reading or hanging out alone. Baking, crafting, taking a class or going to a museum or something. Sounds like you're maybe the same. Comfortable with your own company."

Nothing from him. What's up with his cheekbones? They're so angular. And his eyes are this incessant shade of blue. Talk about too much. Pretty people are the worst.

I pick at the paint on the iron bars. It keeps my hands busy. "You know, according to what you said, you don't actually need me."

"How do you figure that?"

"The epidemiologists said *almost* everyone would die," I say. "There are three hundred million people in this country. So your figure of ninety-nine percent still allows for a few hundred thousand to survive. That's a lot of people. I guess some will be immune and others are hiding in bunkers or whatever. Prepping has been big for ages. They must be so excited to finally get to eat canned food and live in a hole in the ground."

"I don't know." His hands don't stop with their smooth rhythm. Thump, thump, thump. "When the alternative is dying miserably from a juiced-up version of the common cold, I would happily eat canned food in a hole."

"You have a point. But we still don't know if that's what's happening." I go back to pacing. "Do you think it's a biological weapon that escaped some secret lab or Mother Nature calling a halt to our bullshit or what?"

"Not a clue. We don't even know exactly who Patient Zero is. Two cases seemed to present at the same time. One in Asia and one in Europe. And it's not like the one in New York was far behind. Where this thing originated is still a damn mystery."

"Hmm. But back to the point I was making about you not needing to keep me safe."

"I am listening," he says.

"By your own reckoning, even in the worst-case scenario, thousands of people are going to survive this. There will be others out there for you to be friends with. Many of them like-minded, forwarded-thinking souls such as yourself. Companions far better suited to the task of living in the post-apocalyptic landscape that you believe our once great nation will become. And this is wonderful news, because you can open the cage door and set me free. Which is, in essence, setting *yourself* free from the staggering burden of the immense amount of guilt and shame you've placed upon yourself by doing this deeply and profoundly shitty thing to me.

"Dean…no one even needs to know this happened. We can just keep this whole awkward situation between you and me forever and ever, the end."

He stops hitting the speed bag. "That was an impressive speech. It's good that you're thinking strategically about this."

"Thanks."

"Still not setting you free."

"Oh, for fuck's sake. Why not?"

"You'd last five minutes without catching it, out of that cage," he says.

"I am not your responsibility. I am not your *anything*."

"We need to start talking about what happens when we leave here."

"You mean in your imaginary world where it's okay to take me prisoner because everyone else is about to die?"

"That's the one. You're getting worked up again, aren't you?" he asks. "Just breathe, Astrid. Everything is okay."

"Bullshit it is." I close my eyelids tight and think calm thoughts for a minute. It mostly works.

"When we leave here, we're going to wait until things have quieted down and the chances of us crossing paths with anyone are unlikely." His cell chimes over on the sofa and he picks it up.

"Update from your friend?"

"Yeah." His dark brows draw down. "Her, uh, wife passed during the night, and she's started showing symptoms. *Fuck.* They were going to have a child. She was so excited."

This stops me. And if he's lying, then the man deserves an acting award, because his expression is honestly kind of gutted. "I'm sorry."

"She knew it was a risk to carry on working. I told her they needed to isolate. But she was always big on duty and getting the job done, you know?" He frowns and sets the phone back down. "Like I was saying…once most of the people are gone, it'll be safer. I know it sounds callous, but it's the truth. We know the virus needs a live host and it only lasts an hour or so on surfaces. But what we *don't* know is if there are people who are immune—"

"You're thinking they could be carriers, like Typhoid Mary. People who have the virus and pass it on despite not showing any symptoms."

"Yeah. If that's what the situation evolves into, things are going to get brutal." His face is hard when he looks at me. "But I'll keep you safe."

The White House appears on the TV with the flag flying at half-mast. Then a serious-faced woman with white skin and blonde hair stands behind a podium, making an announcement. Words I never imagined seeing appear onscreen.

"The President has died from the virus," I repeat dully.

Dean picks up the skipping rope. "My imaginary world seems to be getting more real by the minute."

I shove my shaking hands into my pants pockets. *No. Just no.* Denial is my new best friend. Because this cannot be happening. There's no way the world is fucking falling down around my ears.

Deep, even breaths. Again.

I wonder, if I annoy him enough will he release me? It's honestly worth a go. The idea that he might hurt me doesn't hold water. He just doesn't seem the type. Though I didn't think he would kidnap me and keep my prisoner, so what do I know? Not a damn thing, as it turns out.

"Why not just chain me to something instead of building this?" I ask.

He keeps on skipping. "The cage is safer."

"And this house is where you want to live after everything goes boom?"

"No. Leaving the city will be necessary to get away from the dead."

"Because they'll be zombies?"

He gives me so much side-eye. "Because they'll be breeding diseases and smelling fucking awful. The cities are going to turn into graveyards."

"Where are you thinking of going?"

"Cabin in the woods. Somewhere we can aim to be at least partially self-sufficient."

"I would make the worst fucking tradwife. Just awful. You get that, right?"

He just laughs. *Ugh.*

"So just to reiterate, there's no special person in your life who might perhaps, oh, I don't know, *voluntarily* stay with you during the apocalypse?"

"Nope."

"I wonder why."

His smile is there and gone in an instant. Nice to know he appreciates my wit.

"You do realize I have no survival skills?" I grab hold of the bars, balance my weight on my heels, and swing back and forth. "Or nothing you'd classify as such."

"What skills do you have?"

"Well…I can match separates."

He stops with the skipping and cocks his head. "Separates?"

"Items of clothing. Like tops and pants and stuff."

"Ah."

"I am amazing with a curling wand. And I can track shit down on the internet like you wouldn't believe. Seriously. My shopping skills are top tier. The amount of stuff I've found for friends on sale. But I assume the internet won't survive the downfall of humanity, so…"

"Probably not," he agrees. "What else you got?"

"I am quite good with a cocktail shaker. Not bad with a madeleine pan. But where I really shine is supporting the recently dumped by talking smack about their ex. Though that has bitten me on the ass a couple of times, because they've gotten back together after I said some things. So awkward."

"That must suck."

"You have no idea," I say.

Nothing from him.

"I kind of want to kill you."

He laughs. "You realize you're hurting your argument with the threat. There I was, starting to fall for your bullshit and see you as nothing but a liability. But keeping you behind bars just seems wise now."

"I've never actually wanted to physically harm someone before. Not really."

"No?"

"No," I say with wonder.

He nods his head. "I am honored."

"We all say we want to do things like that now and then. It's like a throwaway line that doesn't mean anything. But *you*…"

Loud banging sounds come from somewhere. Dean's smile falls from his face, and he turns his head to track the noises. Next is the roar of a car engine and the spinning of its wheels disappearing into the distance. The following silence is deafening.

"Was that a gun?"

"Yeah," he answers. "I am not going to let anyone hurt you. You have my word."

I don't know what to say. In a rare moment of wisdom, I shut my mouth and sit my ass back down on the mattress. This is a lot. Just the whole situation.

He watches me for a moment in silence. Then he says, "All of the things that you think aren't skills…you know how to live, Astrid. Do you even realize you go around with a smile on your face most of the damn time? You are basically a happy person who knows how to make the most of your life. That's something I can honestly say, after four decades on this planet, I still don't have the hang of. But I am really hoping you can teach me."

CHAPTER THREE

SATURDAY

NEWS CHANNELS ARE NOW REPORTING THAT THE hospitals are overrun. People are being directed to camps set up in parks and parking lots by FEMA. Our current President is the Secretary of Defense. Sixth in the line of succession. Seems the virus is moving faster now, laying waste to the population and life as we know it at an alarming rate.

This is real. It's actually happening.

The other big news of the morning is how someone has blown up the Golden Gate Bridge. Hopefully Mom and Dad were nowhere near when it happened. Our military might have done it to slow down the exodus of sick people from the city. But it doesn't seem to have happened elsewhere, and no one is laying claim to the deed. On the other side of the country, parts of the Eastern Seaboard have lost power.

No corner of the world has remained untouched by this disaster. Paris is rioting, Johannesburg is burning, and a nuclear power plant has exploded in Iran. Though some are saying it was a missile strike with some country using the chaos of the pandemic as cover.

And that's not the only place where there's talk of war. Various hands are apparently hovering over the nuclear codes. Like bombs are going to make anything better. Hard not to believe we aren't doomed.

I think I'm in shock. It's like there's this increasing edge of panic to everything. There's a bruise on my arm from where I pinched myself to check that this is not, in fact, a dream. It's quite a big bruise. I may have pinched myself several times. Because I would really like to wake up from this particular nightmare.

Meat loaf with corn bread and collard greens were for dinner the night before. Peach cobbler is for breakfast. The man can cook. I think he's half showing off his skills. Trying to sell me on what a great catch he'd be—post-apocalyptic husband-wise. Guess he's really hoping for Stockholm syndrome to kick in. And the other half is him making the most of modern amenities while we still have them.

We heard gunshots several more times through the night. Along with the horrible sound of someone screaming in the early hours of the morning. I made Dean call the cops, but he said he couldn't get through. All of the emergency lines were jammed. No idea if he was telling the truth.

He slept on the sofa. Said it was in case I needed anything, but it definitely had more to do with keeping an eye on me in case of some sort of shenanigans. Every hour or so he went upstairs to make sure the house was secure. To walk the perimeter, as they say in the movies. There's been no sign of the police or anyone vaguely interested in rescuing me. And as much as I would like to slay my own monsters and heroically save myself, no ideas or opportunities for same have appeared.

My meals are passed through the bars. He's never unchained the door panel to my cage. Not while I was conscious, at any rate. Testing the welded joints of the iron fencing with my body weight has gotten me nowhere. In the bathroom is a small window up high. But he's covered it with some sheet metal and bolted it into place. Pity I didn't think to hide a drill or pry bar in my hair.

It would seem he's thought of everything.

I am stuck.

He's busy doing push-ups today. By the time the world falls apart—*if* the world falls apart—he's going to be in even better shape. Not that I'm noticing him in a physical way. How weird would that be?

"That's about the last of the British royal family," I say, pointing the remote at the TV to change the channel. He handed it over an hour or so ago. I think it was to distract me from my anxiety. Watching the world slowly self-destruct from a distance can get you down. Though I am still not completely convinced humans won't somehow come out on top. We're sort of insidious. Us and cockroaches. "Besides the ones that live here. The UK still seems a day or so ahead of us in deaths, if what your friend said is right. You know they plan their funerals years in advance. The royals, I mean. What music and the carriages and the big parade and everything they want. This lot might have to go without all of that, with the way things are looking."

Dean grunts in reply.

Many of the familiar faces are now gone from the screen.

The remaining reporters have an air of grim determination. Like they're committed to seeing this through to the bitter end.

I don't want to believe this is going to be as bad as my captor is saying. Only a few hundred thousand of us left rattling around in this country. But it seems far more viable today than it did yesterday. Which is fucking terrifying.

"This should solve climate change, at least," I say.

Dean snorts. He is such an animal. And yet I am the one in the cage. Make it make sense.

I saw something interesting when he handed over the remote—a bunch of small round scars on the inside of his arm. About the size of burns from a cigarette. He mentioned getting blown up while in the Marines. They could be to do with that, but somehow I don't think so. I don't want to empathize with him. Though it does make me wonder about his childhood. He said he didn't have any family.

Which just goes to show how a man will kidnap you and take you prisoner rather than go to therapy.

And back to the flat screen. Weather reports don't seem so important when you're being detained in someone's basement and can't go outside. I skip to the next channel.

It all happens so quickly.

The familiar handsome man with neat, short silver hair and a lean, lined face with white skin picks up a grenade. He gives the camera a final nod. It's a comradely one of respect and acknowledgment. Then he pulls the pin.

In no time at all there's the roar of the explosion and the screen goes dark.

My jaw just falls open. "Fuck."

"Yeah."

"This can't…" I say. "You have to have…"

"Astrid, you know I am not faking this. People getting sick, things shutting down…it all started days before I put you in that cage."

And he's right. I know he's right. This is no elaborate ruse.

"I need my phone," I say, not for the first time. The thought of not seeing my family again won't leave me alone. And the fear is real, far more so now than before. "*Please.* You said we'd talk about it later. But you weren't interested in discussing it last night. So how much later did you mean? I just want to check that my mom's okay."

"She won't be. Everyone we've ever known is dead or dying. I'm sorry."

"Then at least let me tell her I'm okay." I scowl. "I need to hear her voice again. I won't say anything about you. Just that I'm safe. Please!"

With a grim expression, he stands and fetches my phone from beneath some papers and other assorted stuff on the coffee table. The fucking thing was right there all along. Just a few feet away from me. This asshole.

He turns it on and holds it up to the bars so it can recognize my face to dismiss the security screen. Then he kneels down in front of the cage. "I'll call your mom and put her on speaker."

"Okay."

"The second you say anything that could put us in danger, I disconnect the call."

I kneel down in front of the iron bars. "Understood."

First comes the ringing. It goes on and on until the call rings out. He immediately tries again, and this time my mom picks up.

"Astrid? Sweetie?"

"Mom," I say with relief.

"We've been trying you for days."

"I am sorry. I got caught up with work and everything that's been happening," I say. "Didn't mean to make you worry. Are you okay?"

She pauses to cough—and my stomach sinks through the floor. "Your dad and I are fine. Just a touch of that flu that's going around. But we don't have it bad like those other poor souls."

"Oh. That's, um, that's good."

"We probably caught it at pickleball on Friday. But we won the game, so it was worth it!"

"I thought we agreed you weren't going to go to that."

"Oh, sweetie," she says. "If it was safe enough for you to pop out to buy groceries, it was safe enough for us to go get some exercise."

And the compassion in Dean's gaze just might wreck me.

Say he released me now, and I got in my car and drove. All of the ways out of the city are clogged with people who were trying to flee the virus. There's been footage of the dead sitting in their cars, caught in traffic forever more.

But say I found a way around it all and got out of the city. San Francisco is a ten-hour drive. I don't have enough gas in the car and no idea if the gas stations are still open. Though siphoning from the tanks of the recently deceased would work. So, say I managed to get all the way there and I'm in time. Miracle of miracles, Mom and Dad and my brother and his wife are all still alive. I nurse them through their last moments. I get to be there and hold their hands and tell them I love them to their faces.

Of course, I've then been exposed to the virus also and will soon be dead.

The end.

"Your brother and Emily were over last night to check on us," says Mom. "They brought homemade soup. It seems like everyone has a touch of it. Don't get me wrong, flu season is awful every year. But this time it's just running wild."

"Yeah."

"But you don't sound congested," she says. "That's good."

"I've managed to dodge it so far."

"Wonderful. Make sure you wear your mask if you go out and keep washing your hands, won't you?"

"Mm." I try to smile so she can hear it in my voice. But I can't stop the tears from falling down my face. "Tell me about your pickleball win."

I don't know what to do with myself. I am sad and hurt and angry. Both at Dean and myself and at the world at large. What I should have done is push to call Mom sooner. But it's not like I took the virus seriously until now. They had supplies; there was no need for my parents to go out. She'd given me her word they'd stay safely at home. Pickleball, of all fucking things. Though it's not like I was any better—leaving the safety of my apartment in search of cake. Would I be dead now had I gone shopping?

Probably.

Mom and I talked for half an hour. That's when she began to worry something was wrong. Guess I sounded maudlin, going over old memories and so on. Like my captor said, my personality is generally sunshine. Something proving hard to maintain under current conditions. Mom cut up carrots, apples, and ginger for a juice while we spoke. It's her fix for the virus. How I wish it were so easy.

I told her I loved her, and I told my dad, too. There's not much else I can do. And I hate being so helpless.

By the time we say our goodbyes, my eyes are swollen and red. I can only hide out in the bathroom for so long without it being obvious. For some reason, I care what my captor thinks of me, apparently. So I take a shower and wash my hair and have a cry. Just get it all out. Then I wash my panties and bra with soap and water in the sink and hang them over a towel rail to dry. Next, I braid my hair into a crown to keep my fingers busy for a while. The world is ending, so I am doing my hair. How ridiculous.

But what are you supposed to feel when everyone you know is dead or dying? When society is taking its last gasping breaths? Feeling like shit seems a reasonable answer, to be honest.

One of my earliest memories is of getting bitten on the toe by an ant. Strange but true. Mom was busy gardening in the backyard, but she gave that ant a good scolding, making me laugh. And I remember my dad coming home from a business trip one time with a huge smile on his face. He'd brought me this stuffed toy from Alaska. It was a seal, and we named it Roger for some reason. Most of the childhood memories of my brother involve us fighting. We outgrew it eventually and get along well now.

I thought there'd be time for more moments. Chances to make memories. No doubt everyone feels that way. But one day your time is up and there's nothing you can do. There's no bartering or arguing or holding back death.

My friend Thu was getting married in June. And another

friend, Sage, was expecting their first child in August. I'd been saving up for a summer holiday. Though I hadn't gotten around to deciding where. There were so many things I was going to do someday.

Which is when I smell it…there's smoke in the air.

"It's a house down the block," says Dean, as soon as he sees me. The worried expression on my face is apparently obvious.

"Is the fire department there?" I ask. "I didn't hear any sirens."

"No. There's no sign of them. Just some people working with hoses to put it out."

"Are you going to help?"

"I don't know if they're coughing from the virus or smoke inhalation. But we can't risk exposure," he says matter-of-factly. "We had a good amount of rain earlier in the week and the wind is in our favor for now. Let's just wait and see what happens."

Stacked storage boxes sit at the back of the room. This is the first time he's shown any interest in them. He takes down the top one and pops the lid. Out comes a backpack, which he sets down in front of the cage. This is exactly what I need. A distraction so I can pretend everything isn't going to hell.

"This one's yours," he says, undoing the zips.

"Nice color."

"You wear a lot of blue." He shrugs. And it can be nice to be noticed, but not so much when it comes with a side of stalker. But here we are. "I was hoping we'd have more time to talk."

"More time for you to convince me to be your apocalypse wife?"

He proceeds to set the items from inside the backpack into neat rows on the ground. "It's important you know what you have in your pack. N95 face masks, hand sanitizer, toilet paper, menstrual products, wet wipes, toothbrush and toothpaste, soap and a towel, hairbrush and hairbands, deodorant, lip balm—"

"Is it flavored?"

"No."

"Good."

"A basic first-aid kit including ibuprofen and a few other over-the-counter medications, rain poncho, an emergency Mylar blanket, spare pair of wool socks, a hoodie in case you get cold, a bottle of water and a water bottle with a filter built into it, a few granola bars, some packets of trail mix, flashlight, emergency light sticks, matches, a lighter—you can use a tampon for tinder to start a fire if necessary—a walkie-talkie already set to the same channel as mine in case we get separated, extra batteries for the flashlight and walkie-talkie, and this—"

"You've put a lot of thought into this."

"Not really. Standard bug-out bag. There's also this…" What he pulls out of the backpack looks like if a hatchet, a hammer, and a pry bar had a baby. And that child chose to be shiny and sleek. "This multitool is what you use to gain access to any locked home or building for shelter or supplies. But remember, we don't know who's out there or how dangerous they might be."

"Yeah. They could be the kind of person who kidnaps you and sticks you in a cage."

"Or they could be a whole lot fucking worse. How many people are going to keep being polite once laws go by the wayside?"

"Joke's on you, because the bulk of them weren't polite in the first place." I hold out my hand through the bars. "Can I see that?"

"No," he says.

"Why can't I have a look at it?"

"Because it would be incredibly sad if you killed me accidentally or otherwise."

I sigh. "Would it, though? Would it really?"

"Think about the situation we're in. No one official has come to deal with that fire. Whoever's left is either too sick or doesn't care. What do you think the chances are the cops are doing any better? It's going to be dangerous. You need to take this seriously."

I say nothing. There's nothing to say.

"If we go out there…*when* we go out there…being quiet is best. So no smashing glass or making a ruckus unless you can't avoid it, okay?"

"Okay."

"And trust nobody. I don't care how nice they seem. Don't approach anyone and don't allow anyone to approach you," he says in his deep voice. "I can't keep you locked up forever. Not if we want to have a decent quality of life. And handcuffing you to me would just be a damn good way to fuck up and get the both of us killed. But you and me, watching each other's backs, being as careful as we can be. That's how we survive this and stay alive.

"I know this has been horrible for you. You've got to be scared and traumatized and I don't know what else. But I wouldn't have done this if there'd been any other answer. Any other way for both of us to get safely through this first stage of everything collapsing."

I may not like it, but the man is talking sense. All evidence points to this being the end times or something seriously close to same. "Alright."

"Good." He gives me a long look. "You're making a run for it the second you get a chance, aren't you?"

"You want an honest response to that?"

"Please."

"I haven't quite decided. Thinking this might be more of a wait-and-see situation."

He raises his dark brows. "That's honestly a better response than I expected. Anyway…it's good for you to give it some thought."

"You want me to think about running away?"

"Yes," he says. "I want you to think about it hard and think about it now. Not after you've done it and you realize what it's going to be like to be alone in this world. You know what Thomas Hobbes said about a world without the rule of law?"

"Who's Thomas Hobbes?"

"Philosopher. He said that life would be solitary, poor, nasty, brutish, and short."

"Sounds like a cheerful guy. What did he have to say about kidnapping your neighbor?"

"I don't remember him saying anything about that. But he was a realist," says Dean. "I don't think your life would be solitary, though. You're an attractive woman. There'll be plenty of men in this new world you won't want to meet on your own."

"So you're the best worst alternative?"

He snorts. "Something along those lines."

"Do you remember that news channel ever being off the air?" I pick up the remote off my mattress. On the TV is gray fuzz. "That's not even the one where the dude detonated himself."

"No. Never."

I change the channel. The next one has a reporter sneezing

into a wad of tissues while announcing how a countrywide state of martial law has been declared. There will be a seven o'clock curfew enforced to help stop looting and the spread of the virus. And this is all ever so slightly fucking alarming.

"There go our rights, apparently," I say.

"Bound to happen eventually. Wonder if they have enough soldiers still standing to enforce it." He puts the backpack on the sofa and takes down another storage box. From out of this one come thick pillar candles and matches. "We're going to lose power sooner or later. Best to be prepared."

"When did you order all of this stuff?"

"Start of the week."

"You knew that early?"

"The conversations my friend was overhearing…they weren't good." He arranges the candles on the coffee table and then heads for the stairs. "I am going to go check on the fire."

"It's a week today since we first heard about this thing. You'd think it would take longer than seven days to bring about the complete and utter downfall of civilization."

"Not really." The edge of his mouth inches upward. "We were never as important as we thought we were."

I get comfortable on the mattress once more. "Guess not."

CHAPTER FOUR

SUNDAY

FORTUNATELY, THE FIRE DOESN'T BURN DOWN THE neighborhood during the night. The local neighborhood watch crew get it under control and we're safe for now. But disasters, natural and otherwise, are befalling the country. Take the jumbo jet crash-landing in the middle of Manhattan. Or the gas tanker exploding and taking out a chunk of Peoria. And the storm about to make landfall in the Florida Keys is terrifying. Not everyone is dying of the virus and no one is coming to help us. Which is a lot of non-cheerful news before coffee. And I really need coffee.

I didn't sleep well, tossing and turning. Then, when I finally did get to sleep, I dreamed of my family and woke up crying. The urge to crawl into a ball, pull a blanket over my head, and try to ignore everything is strong. Just rot in bed and let the world end without me.

The other event this morning is finding the neat piles of my belongings sitting within reach of my cage. "Oh, good. You've been going through my underwear. You know that normally happens *before* kidnapping, right? There's an order to how these things escalate. It's like Stalking 101."

Dean is standing in front of the TV. "I went over to your place last night to grab a few things. Thought you might be ready for a change of clothing."

"Was anyone around?"

"No," he says. "I heard one of your neighbors coughing inside their apartment, but didn't see anyone. I don't think many people are left now."

"Does that mean you're going to let me out?"

"Let's just wait and see."

Which means no. *Asshole.*

He's left me a coffee in a takeout cup as per usual. Breakfast this morning is overnight oats with blueberries. The reporter on-screen has dark circles beneath her eyes and her hair is tied back in a loose ponytail. This is probably the first time the news of the day has been given by a woman in a Dolly Parton tee. I, for one, salute her taste in music, even if it does portend the end times.

It's hard to understand what I am seeing at first, what they're showing us…the footage is blurry and the camera is shaking. But soldiers are shooting at unarmed people out after curfew. Just gunning them down on the street.

This is incomprehensible. Like something out of a movie.

"Guess they had people still standing to enforce it after all," says Dean unhappily.

"They killed them. They just killed them."

"Yeah."

I shake my head. "Maybe we deserve to get wiped out. It's getting hard not to notice that we kind of suck as a species."

"Humans aren't a monolith, Astrid. We have good and bad.

Don't give up on us just yet." He clears his throat. "I had a look at your place, but you don't seem to own any sensible footwear. The Converse were about the best I could find."

"Excuse me. I have great taste in shoes." I reach for the coffee with a shaking hand. This whole situation, grief over my family and friends, is getting to me. "And are you seriously planning on us hiking all the way to this idyllic cabin in the woods?"

"No. But we may need to do some walking and possibly climbing to get around traffic jams and so on."

He'd made sensible choices when it came to my clothing. Another pair of jeans and a couple of tees. Several pairs of my thicker, less decorative socks. Besides the clothes, there's a couple of books off my bedside table, and a selection of photos of my friends and family. The ones I had hanging on my apartment walls. He ditched the frames and put the pictures in a waterproof bag for me.

It was a considerate thing for him to do. But here I am, still sitting in a cage, so I'm not saying thank you on principle.

Strange how my life can be reduced to just these few meaningful things. There's an apartment full of stuff I've collected across the street. How much would I take with me when it comes down to it? That's the question.

The reporter is busy repeating headlines from earlier when the TV dies. Same goes for the light on the ceiling. With the windows covered, we're completely in the dark down here.

Dean appears a moment later with a flashlight in his hand. He fetches a small camping lantern from one of the storage boxes and passes it to me through the bars. Then he goes about the process of pulling the soundproof padding off the high windows to let in the sun. Guess he's no longer worried about me yelling for help. Perhaps he figures there's no one out there who cares.

"I wonder if the power will ever come back on again," I say.

"Not all of it. Or not for a long time. The world's going to look very different for a while. I'd say a few generations at least."

The sound of tires screeching comes from outside as some maniac races down the road. It's accompanied by shouting and gunshots. Seems someone is having fun running wild. Nice to know the end of times isn't getting them down.

"I can't do much about the TV," he says. "But would you like a lesson in stripping and cleaning a gun?"

"You'd trust me with a gun?"

"An unloaded one. Sure."

And I don't know why, but I laugh until I cry.

MONDAY

Rapunzel got a tower with a banging view. It's safe to say I am pretty damn sick of this basement. On day four of my imprisonment, I am not in the best of spirits. It feels a lot like this dying world is kicking the shit out of me. Hard to be happy when the world is spiraling. I want to ask Dean to call my mom again. But what do I do if she doesn't answer? What then? How do I live through that, knowing she might be gone?

Life is so fucking fickle. It's just one moment to the next with another bill to pay and more tasks to do. The eternal bullshit quest to be the best adult you can be. Telling your people you love and appreciate them barely even ranks on the list of things to do. When the truth is it's the most important thing of all. And how heartbreakingly obvious it is once it's too late.

It's midmorning when he finally makes his appearance in jeans, boots, and leather jacket, carrying a gun on his hip. This is new. While he's had weapons around, this is his first time wearing one. I don't want to be attracted to the asshole, but it's an aesthetic that suits him. I have long since drunk the coffee and eaten the lemon scone he left for me, brushed my hair and teeth, and settled in to read. I assume he baked before we lost power and used a propane burner for the caffeine.

His absence today has made me curious as heck. And I can smell smoke again, which is making me nervous. There's something in the air. I don't know how else to explain it. But the vibes are off.

"How close is the fire?" I ask before he can get a word out.

"It's the police station a couple of blocks over."

"Shit."

From out of his back pocket he pulls a key. "Get your shoes on and grab whatever you want to bring with you. But bear in mind we're traveling light."

"We're leaving right now?"

He nods and draws the chain through the panels of fencing that have been keeping me imprisoned. I, meanwhile, do as told and deal with my socks and shoes. Any chance to get out of here is a very good thing. The sky-blue backpack is deposited beside me on the bed, and I add the photos and a few other items. Though he'd put a lot in the bag, it still weighs more than I expected.

"It's bulletproof," he says, reading my frown correctly.

"Oh."

This is really happening. He's not playing with me and giving me false hope. I am actually getting out of here. The gap in the cage where the fencing swings free like a door seems like an illusion at first. Something I wished and dreamed into being. But then I am stepping through, and thank fuck. Finally out of the cage. It feels like I'm taking my first real breath in days. Freedom, you beautiful bitch.

However, there's a distracting tension to Dean. His movements are hurried as he ushers me up the stairs. He picks up another black leather jacket from the back of a chair that screams single white heterosexual male. One of the great ugly recliners of our time. No doubt he has spent years watching football or whatever in the hideous piece of furniture.

And the front door is right there. Like a dozen steps would see me standing in front of it, and then grabbing the doorknob and dashing out into the open air and away from him forever more. It is so tempting.

"Put it on," he says, handing me the jacket.

"What's happening?"

"Some people are working their way up the block breaking into houses, looking for stuff to steal."

"Are they sick?"

"I don't know, and we're not hanging around to find out."

"You don't want to defend the house?"

He shakes his head. "Getting into a gunfight would cause a whole lot of noise and bring us attention we don't want. Staying here was never the aim. We're just leaving sooner than expected."

I nod as he does up the zip on my jacket. "Okay."

"We're going through to the garage, getting on my motorcycle, and then getting out of here. That's the plan."

"Got it."

"Are you sure about that?" he asks, staring into my eyes.

"Yes."

He takes my hand and leads me through his house. It's the first time we've touched, apart from the small matter of an abduction. "Put a mask on and let's go."

"You said a mask wouldn't help with the virus."

"Yeah. But dead bodies can be a breeding ground for all sorts of shit."

The décor in his living room is sparse. Some scenic framed photos and books. So many books. It almost makes me think better of him. One lone, sad, wilted potted plant that has a definite case for neglect. Not much else is here. It would seem he actually made an effort downstairs with the rug, cushions, and throws for me. Which is kind of both sweet and strange.

Having a stalker isn't quite what I thought it would be like. Not that I ever gave it much thought.

In the garage sits an oversized truck with his name and number stenciled on the door. The man wasn't lying about being a contractor. And a gleaming Triumph motorcycle with saddlebags or whatever they're called, packed and ready to go, also awaits us as promised.

He grabs a helmet off a workbench and carefully puts it on me. Then he does his own in a far hastier manner. Blood pounds behind my ears. It's all I can hear. Boom, boom, boom. He gets on the motorcycle far more gracefully than me. Like he's done this a thousand times or more.

"Arms around my middle," he says. "Hold on tight. Real tight. And don't let go."

After endless days of waiting, this all seems to be happening in an instant. I clasp my hands around his hard body. Touching him, and being this close to him, is weird. But whatever it takes to get out of here.

The motorcycle roars to life, vibrating beneath me. Then the garage door rises, sunlight pouring into the space, dazzling my eyes. Dean guns the engine and off we go, down the driveway and out onto the street.

I don't know if going with him is the best idea. However, until I know more, it feels like the only viable one.

Nothing about the neighborhood is quite how I remember. The world has drastically changed in the four days I've been in a cage. Neglect and despair have settled in and made themselves comfortable. How has everything fallen apart so quickly?

It's more than the trash strewn across the asphalt. Graffiti covers a garage door, and someone's smashed the windshield of my Prius.

There's a body hanging out of the open driver's-side door of an SUV sitting in the middle of the street. An actual real live dead body. The first I've ever seen, but I am sure it won't be the last. Swollen limbs and the stench of rot. The rats and crows have more than the overturned bins to choose from now. What a feast.

It's one thing seeing the desolation from a safe distance on the TV. Up close and personal it's pure, unadulterated horror.

Shouting comes from behind us, followed by the sound of gunshots. Like we're not just leaving the place for them to raid. What more do they want?

It's a tight turn at the corner and then we're speeding down the road, away from the house. Dean knows what he's doing. He maneuvers us around obstacles with ease. So many of the vehicles are occupied by the dead. This is so surreal. His solid presence is welcome amidst all of this chaos.

We pass an ambulance embedded in a power pole. The rear doors of the vehicle are hanging open, with bandages and other detritus spread on the ground. I wonder if that's what killed the electricity. There's a beauty to the awfulness of it—seeing our world so undone. Modern art wishes it was this macabre and absurd.

Black smudges on the skyline mark the remnants of fires in the city. The collection of tents in the parking lot of a sporting goods store must have been one of the FEMA camps. And Humvees and a tank are surrounded by bodies in uniform at a military blockade outside a mega mart. Guess there won't be anyone enforcing the curfew. You'd think sick people would head home and seek their beds. But there are plenty of the recently deceased to be seen. Humanity has been decimated by the virus during the days I was kept in a cage.

It's almost as if my mind wants to back away from the sight of bodies. To imagine they're mannequins or dolls or anything but people whose lives were cut short and whose bodies are now rotting in the sun. The shock of it is too much to process.

We're soon heading away from the familiar. Dean uses footpaths and back alleyways when necessary. He must have memorized a variety of routes. Multiple times we're turned around by traffic. Huge clusters of cars sitting silent forever more like a motor mausoleum. But we wind our way through the suburbs, moving farther and farther out. It's like escaping a labyrinth.

My ass is aching when we finally stop at a park on the edge of the south side of town. We haven't seen anyone alive in over an hour. However, he still makes sure to park near a copse of trees so we'll have some cover.

Stretching never felt so good. I roll my shoulders and unzip my jacket. "We got out."

"Yeah," he says, taking off his helmet.

I take off mine too and place it on the grass and, oh yeah. So much better. The air isn't too bad here. You can't smell the dead as strongly since a breeze is blowing and the houses aren't too close. Birds are singing and bees are buzzing. I don't think I realized how much I missed the everyday things while I was stuck down in the basement. The blue sky and fluffy white clouds and so on. Freedom feels real good on me.

Which is when he grips my wrist and presses his pistol into my hand. And the dangerous end is very much pointing in his direction when he says, "The suspense is killing me."

"What?"

"Are you going to shoot me, are you going to run? What'll it be?"

"Are you fucking serious?"

"As a bullet."

"God, you're dramatic."

"I kidnapped you and held you prisoner. What are you going to do about it?"

"Nothing right now. My ass hurts and I'm thirsty. Did it ever occur to you that I had never even seen a dead body before today?" I ask. "That this has all been quite shocking and traumatic, thank you very much? But oh no. There you go, making it all about you and what you want. *Again*."

"You're not going to shoot me."

"Not right now. Maybe later. I haven't decided yet, and

you're not going to rush me." I shake my head. "Not dealing so well with the whole master criminal side of things, are you?"

"Guess not."

"I told you the guilt would get heavy. But did you listen? No."

He grunts and takes the gun from my hand and puts it back in the holster. Then he fetches a bottle of water from one of his saddlebags. "Here."

"Thank God!" calls a strange voice. It's a man's voice. "Please. I need a doctor."

And the gun is back in Dean's hand in an instant.

"Oh, no," I say, my stomach sinking as I back away from the oncoming unwanted visitor.

Because the man is obviously sick. His nose is red and running. Bare feet shuffle weakly through the grass. He's dressed in a pair of striped pajama pants and a white tee. Guess he came from one of the nearby houses.

"If you can just help me get to the hospital."

"Stay back!" shouts Dean.

"Please help me. I've got no one."

"Don't come any closer."

"There's no one left," says the stranger.

"Don't make me do it, man."

But he doesn't stop. Instead, this hopeful, pleading smile appears on his feverish, sweaty face, and he says, "It's okay. Please. If you could just—"

Red blossoms in the middle of his white tee and he stumbles back a step. He stares down at his chest in confusion. Then his knees buckle, and he falls to the ground.

All of the birds fall silent at the shocking sound. The man

doesn't move again. He just lies in the green grass, eyes staring unseeing at the midday sun.

"You killed him. Holy shit." Bile burns the back of my throat. "Okay. You had to. You had no choice. He would have infected us, wouldn't he?"

He holsters the gun and says nothing for a moment. "We need to move. Put on your helmet and get back on the bike."

CHAPTER FIVE

MONDAY

THE NEXT STOP IS A CAMPING STORE IN ONE OF THOSE shopping centers where all of the businesses face outside. And we aren't the first nonpaying customers. Someone drove a sedan through one of the storefront windows for easy access. Dean checks that they're gone while I wait with the motorcycle. He even gave me a gun to hold—just in case.

My growling stomach demands the snacks in my bag. We haven't had lunch, and it's midafternoon. I don't know how I can be hungry after seeing hundreds of dead bodies and someone get shot. I don't know if I am disassociating or compartmentalizing or what. Just doing my best not to think of the sick man and the sound of the gun and the bright red blood on his white shirt.

Today has been a horrible adventure. But I keep my attention on the mostly empty parking lot and the road beyond. No one else is sneaking up on us today. I refuse to spend four nights in a cage, just to get taken out by some random wandering plague victim. Not on my first day out in the world. Which sounds incredibly callous and messed up, even inside my own head. I have at least that level of self-awareness. But it's still a valid concern.

I am not sure I could actually shoot someone. Looking vaguely menacing, however, I can do.

Dark clouds are gathering on the horizon. No idea what the plan is for our temporary accommodation tonight. However, sleeping under the stars is out of the question. The thought of going from house to house, searching for an abode unoccupied by the dead, does not appeal. Death has a smell that seeps into your pores and isn't soon forgotten. Guess we're going to have to get used to it. For a while at least.

The silence is deafening. I noticed it as soon as Dean stopped the motorcycle engine. Birds and insects are still doing their thing, but the human-made noises are gone. Chatter, engines, electronics, and all of the other background sounds we contributed have disappeared. This whole new world seems so empty. Signs of life are few and far between. The raiders we ran from and the infected man in the park are the only people we've seen since starting our travels. It's like we're the only people left alive in this corner of the country.

Now, Dean is back at the smashed window, waving me forward.

"What are we getting?" I ask, always eager for some shopping.

"Decent boots for you. Come on. Watch where you step— you don't want to slip. There're no doctors left to pick glass out of your ass. Only me."

"Yeah. Let's maybe avoid that situation."

He escorts me to the relevant aisle with a hand to my lower back. I don't hate it for some reason. It would seem any uninfected human contact in the apocalypse can be a comfort. And the man has had a hard day, what with having to shoot a complete stranger and all. This doesn't mean I like him or anything. I am, however, able to think rationally about the incredibly messed-up situation. Or at least I hope I am.

There's enough sunlight to see the first half of the store. Then his flashlight comes in handy for the shadowy rest. Whoever went shopping here before us only took what they needed and didn't attempt to trash the place. Which is the right attitude to have. There might not be many of us left to share the current surplus of resources, but there's no need to be a dick about it.

"We should probably talk about what happened." I select a pair of nice blue-and-gray hiking boots. "Oh, these are on sale."

"I think the days of worrying about what things cost are over."

"I just mean the boxes are stacked here instead of out back."

"How about that," he says. "I knew your shopping skills would come in handy."

Happily, they have one last pair in my size. "Do they have thick socks? Wearing these in is probably going to be a bitch."

He hands me a pair of woolen socks from another rack. "We don't need to talk about what happened."

"You killed someone. Um. Those are neon orange."

He blinks, tosses the offensive socks aside, and reaches for another pair. This time they're an acceptable shade of cream. "I eliminated a deadly threat. You're welcome. How about these?"

"Thanks." I sit down and start the process of swapping out footwear. My poor sweet Converse. They have served me well. But if hiking boots will make him happy, then I am willing to play along. For now. There's also a small chance he might have a point about them being sturdier and better suited to this new lifestyle. "I believe it's important that we take the time to process the things that happen to us. Let's be honest. It's not like therapy is going to be as readily available as it used to be."

He snorts.

"I am being serious."

"I know you are, and I appreciate the concern."

"Then come on," I say. "You're the one who wanted me along for the ride, buddy. So talk to me."

He hangs his head for a moment. Then he says, "It's not the first time I've killed someone."

"Oh. When you were in the Marines. I didn't think of that."

"That guy in the park…there was nothing anyone could do to help him. He got a quicker and less painful death than he would have otherwise. I promised I'd protect you. That's a promise I intend to keep." He drops to one knee and tightens the laces on my boots. "How do they feel?"

"Fine. Good. Let's move on to the next topic of conversation," I say. "So what are you actually going to do if and when I want to leave?"

He pauses.

"I know we touched on it briefly the other day, but I feel like it deserves a more thorough and robust discussion, now that we have a minute or two to spare."

He gazes up at me, face shadowed in the low lighting. "You could have just left now, while you were outside alone."

"Would you have come after me?"

It takes him a moment. But eventually he answers, "Yes."

The sigh I dredge up is from the sub-cockles of my soul. "Dean…"

"Only to talk to you. To try and convince you to stay with me a while longer."

"This relationship is so toxic."

"Not to take you prisoner again," he says adamantly. "Okay?"

"What if I announced my intention to leave, and we discussed the situation and still found ourselves at an impasse? What then?"

He swears beneath his breath. Profusely. "Then I would allow you to leave."

"You would *allow* me to leave?"

"Yes."

"That you still think you have any claim on me or my comings or goings is a concern," I say. "But I feel that this is at least a step in the right direction. And you saying it while down on one knee in a pose of supplication doesn't hurt."

"Great."

"Do you have your wallet on you?"

"It's in my back pocket." He cocks his head. "Why?"

"I don't have my purse or my phone. None of the things that used to be so vital. It's a weird feeling being in a store in this situation."

"Your phone is in your backpack," he says. "The network is down, but I thought you might want the photos on there or something. Just don't spend too long on it."

"Why not?"

"We have no easy way of recharging."

"Right." I wriggle my toes inside the new boots. "There's a storm coming. What's the plan for tonight? Are we staying here?"

"No. Other people might stop for supplies. Let me grab some stuff and then we'll go."

I nod and check out the rest of the store. "How long do you think it'll take for everything to fall apart?"

"Not long for this place." He rises. "The broken front window will let in the weather. As for others…it'll depend on how sturdy the building is and how hard the storms hit. Nature will reclaim it all sooner or later."

"Yeah."

He stares down at me…and huh. He really is a prime example of a man. Tall, strong, and handsome. When I dreamed of meeting "the one," he looked a lot like Dean. Guess the whole tall, dark-haired, and handsome ideal has always had me in a chokehold. Half-intelligent things often come out of his mouth. He can cook and shop. Ignore the whole kidnapping-and-caging thing and the man's a miracle. I bet he even knows what to do with his dick.

But after everything he's done, I do believe I have officially shelved all of the lust I previously felt for him. Which would honestly be the smartest decision to come out of me in forever.

"What does that face mean?" he asks.

"I don't think we have any chemistry."

"You don't, huh?"

"No. I mean, I used to be attracted to you from afar," I say. "But I think the combination of your actions and these circumstances have killed it."

"You seem relieved by that."

"Very."

"Okay," he says in a calm voice. "Let me just see something real quick."

"No touching without permission, and I am not giving you permission."

"I hear you. It's been a big day with the raiders and everything. You seeing your first death and dead bodies. I shouldn't have pushed you back at the park. I get that now, and I apologize."

"Okay."

He steps forward, and I step back, and this continues until my back hits some shelving. There's nowhere else for me to go. Our boots are toe-to-toe and he is right there, taking up all of the space. Then he simply stares down at me. I don't know if he's trying to intimidate me or hypnotize me.

"What are you doing?" I ask, because paranoid and curious.

"Nothing. Just looking at you. I'm allowed to do that, right?"

"I suppose so."

There's no expression on his face, but there's this kind of knowing in his gaze. This all-consuming awareness of me. Like I am the only thing in the world that matters to him. The only thing he is thinking about and all that he's living for.

I don't know how to describe it. But it's as if someone finally sees me, all of me, and is willing to accept me for who I am. The good and the bad. Including the frequently weird and occasionally cranky. Not a thing I honestly thought would ever happen. And the way this knowledge settles inside of me is honestly staggering.

Of course, he couldn't just leer at my breasts and eye-fuck me. No. He had to go straight for my soul.

"That's cheating," I say.

"I'm not doing anything," he answers, nonchalant as can be.

"You know exactly what you're doing!"

"Is there anything else you need or want here?"

"I don't know. I'm going to have a look around. Without you."

He hands me a flashlight. "Happy shopping. Just remember we're traveling light."

Out this far from town, the roads are mostly clear. It's easy enough to travel, aside from the occasional crash or stopped car. Turns out his idea for accommodation is a dingy motel on the highway. But this particular place would keep a crime scene investigation team occupied for decades. So many body fluids. No hygiene.

"No," I say from the back of the bike.

"It's temporary, just for one night."

"Still no."

"There are only a couple of cars in the parking lot and the manager's office door is open. Easy access and a roof over our heads during the storm."

Heavy drops of rain start to fall and thunder crashes in the distance to demonstrate his point. Because of course the weather would take his side.

"Five minutes back there was a sign for Aunt Betty's Cottages," I say. "Let's go there."

He hesitates.

"You wanted to learn how to be happier. To live a better life, right?" I ask. "There is no joy to be found in this place, Dean."

And he is absolutely about to keep arguing with me when we hear it—the roar of an engine. Dean turns the motorcycle back on and I wrap my arms around his waist. Before we can go anywhere, however, a luxury sports car races up the highway toward us. Sleek and red and going as fast as can be, with music blaring from its speakers. The person driving waves wildly to us out the window while trying to turn and brake all at the same time.

Which turns out to be a lethal combination at the speed they're doing.

Because the wheels screech and the car rolls. It crashes into a light pole before bursting into flames. The beautiful car is nothing more than a mangled mess. No signs of life come from inside. Even the music has fallen silent.

We both flinch a second later when the whole thing goes boom. Fire warms our faces as the explosion reaches for the sky.

"Fuck me," mutters Dean.

I shake my head. "Did that actually just happen?"

"Yeah. Let's get out of here."

And that's how we wind up at Aunt Betty's Cottages. The property isn't far. Oak trees line the driveway leading to three old but immaculate wooden buildings. One is larger than the others and decorated with a sign saying welcome. Aunt Betty had big feelings about butterflies. They're everywhere. Painted on the welcome sign and rendered in stained glass for the wind chime.

We find the lady herself beneath a brightly colored blanket on the couch in the reception. Deceased. Still wearing her name badge, however.

"Should we bury her?" I ask.

"If we start burying people, where do we stop?"

He has a point.

Spruce Cottage sadly seems to be occupied, but Larkspur Cottage is happily vacant. The keys are hanging on a hook behind the front desk. Lace was also big with Aunt Betty. It is on the blankets, cushions, and curtains. Basically, anything in the cottage that could be decorated with lace has been.

As anticipated, however, the accommodations are scrupulously clean and tidy. There's a small kitchen area with a wooden table and two chairs, a couch, armchair, and coffee table, a big bed, and a bathroom.

Dean says nothing and pulls items out of his pack. Starting with candles and a watertight container full of matches.

When I flick the light switch, nothing happens. He was right about that. But water flows when I turn the tap on the kitchen sink. And a cold shower is better than none at all. Or standing out in the rain and hoping for the best.

"I wonder if the person in the sports car was sick," I say.

"Not everyone is going to die of the virus. Some people are just stupid. And stupid is now a death sentence."

"You never gave in to the impulse to do something wild?"

He shrugs. "I kidnapped and caged you."

"You're amazingly adept at reminding me why I don't like you," I say with a frown.

His answering smile is there and gone in an instant. "I don't do it on purpose. But without society to keep people in line, things are going to fall apart. We talked about this already."

"We discussed it briefly. You really think societal norms were that strong?"

"For some people. Especially when it's backed up by the law. But access to alcohol and drugs, for instance, generally came down to how much money you had. That's not the case anymore. Anyone can throw a rock through a liquor store window now and drown themselves in whiskey without fear the cops will come calling."

"Sad to survive the virus just to go out that way."

"The trauma of watching everyone you know die and having the world fall apart would probably have the most balanced person reaching for a bottle." He scratches at his stubble. "Like you said…therapy is going to be a lot harder to get."

"Mm."

Speaking of which, inside the small fridge are bottles of water, a six-pack of beer, and a bottle of white wine. Aunt Betty knew how to have a good time. For my purposes, the bottle of wine will do just fine.

"If there's a tub, we need to fill it," he says. "And we should start boiling our drinking water."

"Why?"

"Just to be safe. No idea how long the taps will keep working or how long we can trust the filtration systems."

"That makes sense."

"Glad you think so," says the sarcastic dick.

I put my backpack beside the bed, grab my phone out of it, and head into the bathroom with my bottle of wine. There is indeed a tub. Along with a collection of scented oils and bath salts sitting in a basket bedecked with lace.

I start the water running as suggested. Then I shut the bathroom door and get comfortable with my back against it. This is going to hurt and there's nothing to be done about it. Not a single thing. My need to hear their voices matters more than the pain. I grit my teeth, turn on the phone, and watch the notifications fill the screen.

And more than enough messages downloaded onto my

phone before mobile coverage went down to give me my fill of anguish and horror.

Night has fallen and the storm has moved on by the time I leave the bathroom. My head hurts from crying and my eyes sting like a bitch. But Aunt Betty didn't have half bad taste in booze. One bottle of wine, however, was insufficient for the pain. Grieving my family and friends isn't something that's going to go away anytime soon. Right now the wound is raw and fresh. I think time will change how I carry it, but not take it away. Which feels about right for this sort of love.

All of the block-out curtains have been drawn. Guess we don't want to risk anyone seeing a light and coming to say hi. As a woman in the world, I'm used to requiring a certain amount of safety. Being mindful of where I am and what's going on. Carrying a can of pepper spray in my purse and texting a friend the license plate of a rideshare or a date. But this is a whole new level of worry and awareness.

Things sure change fast sometimes.

Dean is seated outside on the swing chair on the porch. I ate the emergency rations bar he slipped beneath the bathroom door several hours ago. Talk about a comedown from his cooking. There's a small CB radio in his lap and he's moving the dial, searching for signs of life. Seems to be mostly static.

I take a seat on the steps. The sky is clear, an endless field of stars. Light pollution is a thing of the past. I stare in wonder at the Milky Way for a good minute or more. It's mind-blowingly beautiful.

"I thought I could protect you from anything," he says. "But I can't protect you from getting your feelings hurt."

I turn and rest my back against the railing so I can see him. He's all shadows in the starlight. Half mystery and half monster. Though those percentages may be off. I honestly have no idea these days. Life has not turned out as I expected.

The man genuinely seems to think he has a connection to me. Like he's been thinking and feeling things about me for a while now. Four days ago, he was the dude with the pretty face who lived across the street. Nothing more. I enjoyed seeing him mow his lawn in the summer. How the muscles in his arms would work. But he was just a passing thought. Hearing him plan for my survival and care about my emotions is so strange. No one has really wanted to look after me since I was a child.

"If you need to be alone to think things through, then okay. But I don't want you to be lonely." He pauses. "What I'm trying to say is, if there's anything I can do…"

"Let's talk about lonely," I say, getting comfortable. "If the plan is to find a cabin in the wilderness somewhere, then what are you searching for on the radio?"

"Where people might be gathering so we can avoid those places."

"Did you find any?"

"No. Not yet. Someone's playing classic rock and a couple of people are talking about safe routes out of Portland. There's an emergency broadcast from the government still playing on repeat, telling people to report to FEMA camps. That's about all so far."

"People aren't organizing communities."

"Not yet."

"Then that's what we need to do."

"What?" he asks in surprise.

"You heard me."

"Yes. I heard you. Now help me to understand why, after everything you've seen today, you would say that."

"Not everyone is going to be feral or infected."

"Those aren't the only dangers to us," he says.

"Dean, has it occurred to you that the reason why you chose me is the same reason why I am not going to agree to live in an isolated cabin in the woods with you?"

He sighs. "You don't think this is maybe a little premature?"

"I think where we settle is going to affect how we go on. And I don't mind spending time on my own, but I'm also a social person."

"You can talk to me."

"Whether or not we can be friends is still up for debate," I say. "It's also beside the point. Humans need community to thrive."

"There has to be some sort of compromise we can make here." The man is not happy. I can feel the grumpy vibes emanating from him on the cool night air.

"Just think about it. We can talk more tomorrow. My head hurts and I'm going to bed."

"There's Advil in your backpack, and don't forget to drink some water."

"Thanks."

Which is when something bursts into flames on the horizon. Far away from us, fortunately. Judging by distance and size, it's probably a building in the city. What is strange is how I am not even particularly surprised by the inferno. How quickly this sort of thing has become the new normal.

Life post-apocalypse sure is something. When the only lights left in the city are the fires raging out of control. Goodbye technology. So long law and order. Farewell government and commerce. Though to be fair, some of those things were fucking awful at times.

"The people doing this are the same ones you want us to try and live with," he bitches.

"You know perfectly well not everyone is like that. I think you're right about there being a second round of deaths, though. The careless and the callous and those who are just shit out of luck."

His response is a grunt.

"Sweet dreams, Dean."

And so ends our first day out in the wilds. With me in the bed, him on the couch, the dead all around us, and the world on fire.

CHAPTER SIX

TUESDAY

WE BID ADIEU TO AUNT BETTY'S AND HEAD SOUTH the next day. I make the bed and leave the dishes clean and packed away in the kitchen cupboard. Ready for any other visitors. Dean probably thinks it's a waste of time. But being respectful feels right, even if we're not burying the bodies.

Both of our future plans require a more temperate climate. Somewhere we can grow fruit and vegetables. California makes sense. We need a moderate winter and a long grow season. There are plenty of canned goods for now, but they won't last forever. It may not be an issue for a decade or two; however, lack of fresh food is bound to get old sooner or later. And I know next to nothing about gardening, so we're going to need to read a library full of books.

Dean says the coast isn't a great option due to tropical storms. Like floods and fires don't happen in other areas. Any place we pick will have positives and negatives. What we can agree on, however, is that we want to settle somewhere with good access to water. And I know just the place.

I woke to find him doing push-ups and sit-ups on the front patio. He sure is determined to face the apocalypse at peak personal fitness. Breakfast was another emergency rations bar and a cup of coffee. Thank fuck for caffeine. I need something to combat the nightmares waking me up every other hour. Mom calling to me from somewhere out of sight. Rooms full of rotting bodies closing in on me. Empty cities echoing with my calls for help. So delightful.

I pop another couple of Advil to combat the lingering headache. From a hangover or crying my heart out—who knows?

One thing I will say, I am getting to see some of the countryside. There's no ticking clock on this adventure. No rush to get anywhere. And no distractions apart from the ever-present existential crisis that is the fear of death. Which has actually sort of loosened up after seeing so much of it. With no hospitals or doctors, we could die at any moment from things that would have been deemed a nonevent a fortnight ago. Hiding isn't the answer to this new threat. So many people didn't get to live. We need to make our days count.

But back to the scenery. They say the world seems different from the back of a bike. It's certainly a nice way to experience the open road. More immediate. Like you're part of the landscape instead of just moving through it. I don't know. Spring wildflowers are starting to appear in all the colors of the rainbow. It's good to see beauty in the world. For the cycle of life to be playing out across the land no matter what nonsense is happening with the human race.

Lunch requires a small camp stove. Dean boils water in a collapsible kettle to make two packets of freeze-dried mac and cheese. You add the water to the pouch, stir it well, seal the packet back up and wait for the magic to happen. And we're doing this underneath a tree in the middle of nowhere.

I can now officially say that touching grass in the middle of an apocalypse doesn't particularly help. However, set aside the grief and stress for a moment, and the peace and quiet sure are something. They do help to soothe the soul.

My traveling partner keeps an eye on the horizon, constantly checking both directions. The man is not the least bit soothed and remains on high alert. His military past is more evident in the way he moves now.

I watch him from behind my black sunglasses. He interests me for some reason. I don't know why. Apparently, as he proved to me yesterday, my awful taste in men has sadly continued on into the end of the world. Life would probably be easier if he were less appealing. Had any and all of my feelings for him truly fucked off into the wide blue yonder. There's still time for them do so, however. Got to be positive.

So far, we've stopped to siphon gas from other vehicles and to pee behind both bushes and a tank. An actual Army tank. Not something I ever imagined myself doing. The way my traveling companion eyed up the tank with such longing... But sporadic signs of the military are to be found even this far from the city. Dean helped himself to some of their guns and other equipment. Stealing from the dead is supposed to be unlucky. Though everything we do from now on will probably involve taking from the dearly departed in one way or another.

I take a sip of water. "Fewer people today."

"Back roads are safer. Just not dirt ones. We don't want to kick up dust that someone could see and use to track us."

"You're still wearing the gun."

"That's probably going to be a permanent thing from now on."

"Should we risk a grocery store?" I ask. "Seems an unlikely place for dead bodies. We could see if there's any fresh produce left while it's still edible."

"I know this stuff isn't great. It's not what I had planned, but we had to leave my place in a rush."

"We have food, and I'm grateful. Really. Just trying to figure things out," I say. "No doctors and nurses means we need to be mindful of our health, right?"

He sits with his back against the trunk of an elm tree. "Given the rate at which this virus works, we should be mostly safe from it within another day or two. By then, anyone who has it should be dead."

"Okay. So we could maybe hunt up some multivitamins and see what else is on the menu, then?"

"Yeah. But we still have to worry about raiders. Like those people who were coming to break into the house. They may have been after more than just stuff. You get that, right?" His forehead fills with furrows. "Some of the survivors will only do what they need to get by. But others will get off on hurting people, and there's no one to stop them now. Not necessarily any consequences to their actions. Someone stealing our shit is one thing. But rape, torture, murder…"

"You're trying to scare me."

"Doesn't make it any less the truth."

"I know." Time to give lunch the taste test. "Cheesy."

"Please tell me you'll be careful and take the threat seriously."

"I will be careful."

"Thank you," he says, stirring the contents of his own

pouch. "I appreciate you sticking with me and giving this a chance."

I smile. "I am not an idiot, Dean. This new world scares the shit out of me."

"You don't show it."

"Bravado is my bitch. But I acknowledge that my chances of survival are better with you than they would be on my own. Though that may change as time goes by. I don't know."

He half smiles and asks, "How'd you end up in Oregon?"

"Followed a boyfriend. Wound up dumping him but decided to stay. Portland had a good music scene. Cool shops and cafés."

He just nods.

"You were never tempted to leave?" I ask.

"Nuh."

We're back to one-word answers. This won't do. "Tell me about your exes," I say.

The way his wary gaze jumps to my face, it would seem I have startled the man. "Why do you want to know about them?"

"Because I want to know about *you*."

Such a heavy frown. Oof. "There were a few. None of them lasted more than a year or so."

"Why is that?"

He shovels a forkful of mac and cheese into his mouth. Such a great way to get around having to answer. But I am patient as can be. When he finally finishes chewing and swallowing, he says, "I don't know."

"Bullshit."

"They wanted more than I had to give."

"There you go." I take another sip of water. "Your commitment issues sure changed quickly."

"Funnily enough, news of the world ending sort of shocked the fuck out of me."

"It's going around." I nod. "How long have you been watching me?"

He sighs. "It wasn't like I was stalking you or anything. I just tended to notice you."

"You don't think this maybe all goes a little beyond tending to notice someone?"

Nothing from him. But his expression is guilty as sin.

"You know, you could have asked me out like a normal person."

"Like I said…I'm not good at relationships. I didn't think I had anything to offer you. And I didn't think that was what I really wanted until any chance of having it was almost gone," he says. "They make you do all these tests when you join the Marines. Not just physical, but mental resilience and emotional stability."

"Okay."

He stares off at nothing for a long moment before saying, "I tend to avoid engaging with things on an emotional level."

"That's the conclusion they came to, huh?"

"Yeah."

"Do you think it's accurate?"

His small smile is as wry as can be. "Don't you?"

"I might have to give that some thought." I eat some more of the mac and cheese. "We need to practice gratitude. It's important for general happiness. Research has shown it reduces stress and can improve your soundness of mind, which seems particularly pertinent to our situation."

"That can't be right," he says. "You're making that up, aren't you?"

"No. Today I am grateful to not have to pay back my student loans. Those predatory interest rates. Such a scam of a system. What about you?"

This small line appears between his brows. "Glad I don't have to worry about medical insurance anymore."

"Yeah. Just out of interest…what are you going to miss?"

"Football." He's such a dude. Honestly. "What about you?"

"Friends and family."

His expression sobers. But his mouth stays shut. What is there to say?

I clear my throat. "I was researching places for a summer holiday with my family. Small towns that were peaceful, heavy on charm and low on people. Not too expensive, though that no longer matters. I found a place called Wolf Creek a couple of hours north of San Francisco. Population five hundred. Not particularly on the way to anywhere important. It's situated between the coastal towns and a wine region."

He cocks his head. "That's where you want to go?"

"I think it wouldn't hurt to take a look."

"Defending a place like that would be a fucking nightmare."

"Would it really, though? Small, with limited entry points? It wouldn't hurt to have some help, however, which is why we need to make friends. Have community."

He gives me a long look. "I am not saying I agree to your

plan. But we have to move in some direction. Guess it might as well be south for now."

I clap my hands. "This is going to be great."

It is not great.

They're perfectly positioned. Waiting for us when we come around a bend on a back road running sort of adjacent to a high-way. Two men stand in front of a large truck that's blocking the road, with another person situated behind it. All of them armed to the teeth, with white skin and short haircuts.

We hadn't seen anyone all day. And now this. None of them seem sick at first glance. In fact, the merry assholes all appear to be in the best of health as they wave their weapons at us in a menacing fashion.

Dean brakes hard, bringing the motorcycle to a stop and sending me slamming into his back. Which is when he hisses at me, "When I give the signal, hit the ground."

There's no time to ask what the signal will be.

"Turn off the engine and throw the keys over here!" yells one of them. And Dean does as ordered.

"Get off the fucking bike!" yells another. "Get your pack and your helmet off."

This cannot be happening. I know stuff has transpired and we've discussed the collapse of societal norms several times now, but yeah. It still somehow comes as a complete surprise. None of them are showing signs of a fever. No coughing or sneezing. And not one of the three seems to have a runny nose. Being this close to them, however, is still one hell of a risk.

I climb off the bike and ease my backpack off. My fingers

fumble over the buckle of my helmet, but I unclasp it in the end and put it on the ground.

One of the assholes walks up to us and grabs me by the arm.

He pulls the mask off my face, looks me over, and announces, "Yeah, she'll do." Which is rude. Then he turns to Dean, looks *him* over, and says, "Drop your piece. Big son of a bitch, aren't you?"

"Drop your piece," I repeat without thought. There is every chance my habit of babbling when nervous is going to get me killed. When my natural state of sarcasm will condemn me. It could even happen today. "Watch a lot of cop shows, do you?"

The asshole smacks me in the cheek, putting me on my ass. "Shut up, you stupid bitch."

It turns out this is the signal. Me getting sucker punched.

None of this would have worked if the asshole who'd hit me had been secure enough in himself to carry a small weapon. But no. He's wielding some huge fucking thing that takes time to bring up and into position.

And by the time he's done that, Dean has already drawn his pistol and put one dead center of his heart. Bang.

I show some intelligence and curl up in the fetal position on the asphalt. Making as small a target of myself as possible. However, I still watch what's happening, because this is life and death playing out in front of me.

Bullets fly on both sides. There are more misses in a gunfight than Hollywood would have you think. And it's loud as heck.

Dean shoots the second asshole standing in front of the truck with relative ease. Just puts one through his face.

But the asshole standing *behind* the truck is a problem. He has shelter.

Dean drops to his knees and aims beneath the body of the beast of a vehicle. And a second later, the last of the three is screaming in pain and then silent as the grave.

"You still breathing?" he asks.

"Yeah." I carefully rise to my feet. Getting punched kind of shook me. No one has ever hit me before. Or not since Hannah Moore, the school bully, in third grade. There's some splatter on me from the guy Dean shot in the chest. So gross. And the sharp scents of gunpowder and the copper of blood are in the air. But I am *not* about to burst into tears or anything. "How about you?"

Before he can answer, I have face-planted in the middle of his chest and am breathing deep. Or at least trying to. However, it takes me a minute to catch my breath, what with all of the sobbing.

He slips his gun back into the holster and pats me awkwardly on the back. Like he has nil experience with comforting a woman in distress. Which actually tracks with his personality and what little is known of his lived experience.

"It's okay. They're not going to hurt you ever again."

I don't actually blow my nose on his tee. But it's a close thing. I take a step back and swipe away the tears and give him two thumbs up.

As for him, he eases off the jacket. Trails of blood are running down his right arm from a wound in his bicep.

I gasp. "You got shot!"

"It went through. Grab your first-aid pack and we'll patch it up before we get back on the road. No idea if these dickheads had friends nearby. They didn't seem sick, at least."

I get the first-aid kit, but before dressing the wound, I say, "We need to get you meds in case of infection."

"I have some antibiotics," he says. "I mean, they're out of date, but they'll do."

"How out of date?"

"Five or so years. They're probably fine."

I raise my brows. "No, Dean. We need a pharmacy."

"Okay." He inspects my face with a frown. "Your cheek is swelling."

"Being mouthy might not have been the best idea in this instance."

"I don't know. As much as I hate you getting hurt, it made for a perfect distraction."

"Great."

"They would have killed me," he says seriously. "You get that, right? What you did was very brave."

"Be honest. We both know perfectly well that it was fueled by idiocy." I don't want to think about what would have happened if they *had* killed him. Nor what they were planning on doing to me. Life sure comes at you hard some days. "Lucky you're a good shot. Now stand still so I can do my nurse thing."

"You do a nurse thing?" he asks with interest.

"Medical-aid adjacent might be more accurate. The worst injuries I've ever treated are blisters from wearing new shoes and a hangnail or two."

He winces. Such a tough guy. "This should be interesting."

I am keeping a mental list of things I wish I had searched for on the internet. Also, losing online maps outright sucks. We still have GPS for what it's worth. Dean said orbiting satellites are constantly bombarding the world with radio waves. He briefly turns on his smartphone and even without mobile data, he can access our coordinates. However, without a connection to a map they might as well be hieroglyphics.

We follow the signs for the closest town. The motorcycle is left on a back street, and we walk the couple of blocks to the drugstore. Then we crouch behind a car in an alley opposite and watch the street for a while.

I've never been on a stakeout before. Or whatever this is. Trash is blowing about, care of a warm wind, and the scent of dead and rotting bodies is in the air. For as long as I live, I will never forget the stench of decay. I wonder how long it takes for a corpse to dry out and desiccate. My life used to be so nice and simple. How the human body decomposed rarely even crossed my mind.

Wherever we settle, we're going to have to deal with the dearly departed. But that's a worry for another day.

Dean's gunshot wound has stopped bleeding. But he's moving in a stiff and careful sort of manner. Like he's in a lot of pain. I have now seen him kill four people. All of them to protect us from the virus or violence. One of these days, I'm going to take a moment to scream into the void. Just get out all of the horror and rage and hopelessness. But there's no time for me to fall apart right now. We need meds and a safe place to stay for the night. Then I'll go back to work talking him into Wolf Creek.

We watch the drugstore for the agreed-upon hour. For safety's sake. I am not great at waiting, but I manage to stay quiet and not fidget too much. I'm happy to be taking a break from the bike. Seems my ass still requires a respite after a certain number of miles. And almost getting kidnapped for the second time tends to take it out of you. Happy to have made it through my first gunfight, too. I feel like you should get a sticker or badge for that.

The drugstore's front window hasn't been broken. You would think this sort of place would be right up there with gun shops in popularity now. I wonder if everyone in this town died. Perhaps the store stayed open until the end and no one needed to steal anything. There's every chance we're the first to visit since the virus shut down this corner of the world.

Though, with that being said, the jewelry store down the street has been broken into. And a body lies on the footpath out front with half of its head missing. Guess a shotgun at close range would do that sort of damage. Though I don't really know for sure. It's just an educated guess care of action movies.

But imagine losing your life over such a thing. You'd get more for a freshly baked loaf of bread than you would for a diamond ring these days. Wander into the right museum and you could bag yourself a crown to wear if you were so inclined. The old ways and wealth are dying a swift death.

Be wild to see if any of the billionaires survived by hiding in bunkers. Their currency and crypto or whatever would be worthless now. All of the tech bros' technology is dead for the time being. Would the former elite still wield any power in this new world, or would they have to content themselves with becoming one of the little people?

There are a couple of cars parked on the street and a

child's bike is lying abandoned on the pavement. One of those with a basket on the front and a bell on the handlebar. I always wanted to get an adult-size one of those.

Dean motions for me to be quiet and to follow. We move swiftly but carefully across the street to the drugstore. After trying to stay still for so long, it feels good to move.

Surprisingly the door is unlocked. How lucky. There'll be no need for breaking glass and making noise. I am looking forward to getting a decent moisturizer for my face and hands. We left the house so fast I forgot to grab one. It's first on my shopping list. Once we've found antibiotics, of course. I wouldn't mind a cold pack for my face, either.

Inside, the air smells of perfumes and body sprays with a strange underlying scent of bleach or something similar. The same as every other drugstore. Familiarity is kind of nice. Like I could close my eyes and pretend the world was still working and all of the people were still alive.

We head straight for the pharmacy area at the back of the store. Both of us take out our flashlights. There's enough sun to see, but not to read the print on all of the boxes and bottles. We head behind the back counter to find what we need.

"We need some stronger painkillers as well," I say. "Just in case."

"I'm going to check out back and make sure we're alone."

"Okay."

Which is when we both hear it—a person hiccupping.

The door of a cupboard is flung open. It's decent-sized and down low. Only a few feet from where I am standing. Out of it flies a young girl. She crashes straight into me, pressing her hot, damp, and snotty face against my tee, and wrapping her arms tight around my waist. And she doesn't just cry, she keens, making this heartbreaking noise.

One that she pauses only to cough.

Dean freezes in place.

CHAPTER SEVEN

TUESDAY

"**D**on't come any closer," I say in my best calm voice.

Dean's expression isn't one I've seen before. His eyes widen for a moment before he can hide the horror behind a blank face. The man is shook. Which is fair enough, since I am feeling it myself.

I smooth a hand over the girl's back, rubbing in gentle circles. Her blonde hair is tangled, her white skin and clothing dusty, and she's overdue for a bath in general. She's between eight and twelve at a guess. I honestly don't know. It's been a while since I've spent quality time around children. Mostly since I was one. But her shoulders are shaking and the front of my tee is sticking wet to my skin. Her face feels so hot. From trauma and grief or the flu, is the question. And honestly, it doesn't even matter all that much. I'm already infected if she has it. There's nothing to be done.

On the other hand, Dean is standing eight or so feet away from us and might not have been exposed. Hopefully not yet.

"Back away," I order him. I stroke the girl's tangled head of hair. "Get out of here. Now."

He stares at the child attached to me with his jaw set. "You don't know for sure, do you?"

"No. But that's beside the point. Until we know, we have to act as if she has it. And that means you putting some distance between us for a day or two to be safe, right?"

He turns his face toward the front of the store. Yes. Saving himself is the good and sensible choice.

"You need to go," I say. But he still isn't going. He's just standing there frowning. "Get out of here, Dean. Now."

"No," he says in this resigned kind of tone, wandering over as calm as can be. "Whatever this is, we're doing it together."

Shit.

He gets down on one knee and pulls tissues and his canteen of water out of his backpack. Then he says to the child, "Here you go."

I am stunned and shocked and all of these things. We're going through some weird times. But for him to bind our fates so firmly together is wild. Don't get me wrong, the man has issues. However, none of them have anything to do with making a commitment to me and our supposed future. Something at which each and every one of my previous relationships spectacularly failed.

No idea how to think or feel about that. Perhaps trepidation for starters, with bewilderment coming up fast.

"What's your name?" he asks. "Are you on your own?"

The little girl allows him to mop up her face. She blows her nose robustly and downs some water. "Sophie. Everybody died."

"My name's Dean, and this is Astrid," he says. "Did you get sick?"

Sophie shakes her head. "Mom did. She locked herself in her bedroom. Told me to stay in the house until the food ran out. Not to let anyone in or talk to them. Just watch my shows or read my books. And I stayed until yesterday. But then the power went out and I got scared."

"I would have been scared too," I say in solidarity. "How old are you, Sophie?"

"Nine."

"Wow. You've been so brave."

Dean nods in agreement. "We're going to need a new plan," he says to me.

And yes, we sure do. But that's how, on the second day of the apocalypse, we become parents.

Neither of us were keen to go from house to house checking on occupancy. And staying in the drugstore seemed too much of a lure for anyone who might be passing and searching for oxy or something. No idea exactly how many were killed by the virus and such. But we've crossed paths with enough people to be cautious.

The home goods store down the block seemed like a good idea for the night. It had a fancy front window display shielding the rest of the shop from view. We only use a couple of small travel lanterns on low setting. And a blanket hangs over the front door to stop any hint of light from escaping.

The town stays quiet as darkness falls. Though howling dogs can be heard an hour or two after. What's happened to all of the pets is a sad thought. But fewer humans will in all likeli-hood be a boon to the rest of the wildlife. It might not be long before whitetail deer and coyotes and who knows what else are common in the streets. More common than people, at least. Weeds and wildflowers will grow through the cracks in the roads and all of our great works will slowly be undone.

I wonder if we're going to live long enough to see it.

Sophie and I are sleeping on the demonstration bed made up with crisp striped linen sheets and fluffy matching coverlets with frilly pillows. Dean will make himself at home on one of a pair of cushioned cane sun lounges. I offered to let him have the bed due to the gunshot wound and all. But he declined.

"You won't leave?" Sophie repeats in her soft, tired voice.

"We won't leave." Dean sits beside the bed on a rustic wooden stool. It's actually quite a nice item. But seven hun-dred dollars for a stool is ridiculous. This place must have had some wealthy weekend visitors to be moving such luxe stock. Don't even get me started on the cost of the French bed linens or the etched glassware. All of it beautiful. The owners, were they still alive, would've definitely looked down their noses at me and my meager budget.

"Promise?" asks Sophie.

"We aren't going anywhere without you. It's okay to close your eyes and go to sleep. When you wake up in the morning, we'll both be right here."

Sophie yawns. "I don't need to sleep."

"Okay."

"The bad guys that hit Astrid and shot you aren't going to find us?"

"No. We will never see them again. They can't hurt any-one else either."

She thinks this over for a while. "What are we going to do tomorrow?"

"Don't know yet," he answers in this low, calm voice. "We can figure it out later. After we've all had some sleep."

"I'm still not tired," she says around another yawn.

"Okay."

I watch from my position on one of the sun lounges. The thermometer in my hand beeps and Dean turns my way. My small smile is answered with a nod from him. Still no sign of a fever and my nasal passages are blessedly free. Sophie has been much the same, though she's done some coughing. Her throat seems irritated, so there's no way to be sure. We're not out of the woods. Not yet.

However, I wouldn't be surprised if she screamed herself hoarse shouting for her mother at the locked bedroom door she told us about.

We gave her throat lozenges from the drugstore. Which were what she'd been there to find. The cough didn't get any worse and no other symptoms seem to have developed. She devoured a packet of the freeze-dried mac and cheese and a packet of freeze-dried ice cream. Weird bunker backpacking food is a win with the child.

We gathered antibiotics and a variety of pain meds from the drugstore. Along with cough medicine and antihistamines and things to see us through the virus if we have it. Wet wipes, multivitamins, and a restock on some items for our first-aid kits were on the shopping list too. Now we wait to see if we're going to die or not. Still waiting.

Sophie's eyelids drift closed ever so slowly. She fights sleep every inch of the way. It's an epic battle. And Dean sits there in silence, waiting her out with infinite patience. His expression never changes, and same goes for his posture. With elbows resting on his knees and his hands clasped loosely together, I would never have picked him as a possible girl dad. But he's shown nothing but this peaceful, pragmatic attitude when it comes to the child. Talk about surprising.

I feel an odd tenderness toward him tonight. Which is also unexpected. No one has ever had my back in this way. Like anything could happen and he would still be standing at my side. It's like the world is daring me trust him or something. Such a wild idea. To be fair…it's not like there used to be multiple life-threatening events per day. But at the end of the world, he is fast proving himself to be the person I need to have with me.

When he eventually comes to join me over on the sun lounges, his frown is heading deep into scowl territory. I am not the only one experiencing big feelings. The last time I saw him this perturbed was the morning he came to tell me people were breaking into houses on the block and we had to flee. He's so emotionally stunted, it's hard to say quite what upset him this time. It could be any one of the several hardships we're currently facing.

"Well done getting her to sleep," I whisper.

"This is fucking terrifying."

"What is?"

"Her."

"The small child has upset you?"

"How do I keep her safe too?" he hisses. "I'm having enough trouble keeping you in one piece."

I bite back a smile.

"It's not funny. Stop smiling. What do we do with her?"

"Our best. How's your arm?"

"Fine," he says dismissively.

"Is this the first time you've been shot?"

"Yeah. Not an experience I'd recommend. Riding in a vehicle that drove over an IED is what got me an honorable discharge."

"Huh."

He relaxes back and kicks off his boots. It takes a few goes, but he gets there in the end. There are bruises beneath his eyes. Like he's in need of some sleep. "I mean, I could probably gradually talk you around to the cabin in the woods. But she's going to need more. Kids her own age. Schooling of some sort. I don't even know what else."

"You could not talk me around," I answer with mild outrage. "And you wonder why I don't trust you."

He snorts. "I don't wonder why you don't trust me. I know full and well why you don't trust me."

"The cabin was never happening."

"It's sure as hell not now."

I shake my head. "Dean, there's something I need to say, and I need you to listen very carefully, okay?"

He turns his head to the side so as to watch me in silence.

"This girl came to me. She trusted me. And if you try to cage one of us ever again, I will react accordingly," I say. "She lives as happy, healthy, and as stable a life as we can possibly provide for her for as long as we're able. Also…I need to learn how to shoot a gun."

"You want me to teach you how to shoot a gun so you can shoot me, if necessary?"

"Yes."

He raises his brows.

"The only acceptable answer to my request is yes. Because you want both me and her to be safe, and teaching me how to defend us makes sense. Especially since those creeps tried to grab me and kill you today."

"I know," he whispers back at me. "But I don't have to like it, Astrid."

My message has been delivered. I allow my attention to take a stroll around the store. "The glaze on those pottery mugs is gorgeous."

Over on the bed, Sophie coughs in her sleep. Dean and I both frown at the sound. Only time will tell if she's sick or not.

"I wonder if we're going to die," I say, just making conversation.

He checks his watch. "It's been eight hours. One of us probably should have started showing symptoms by now if we were going to get it. But…"

"Yeah. I thought I'd be panicking more than this when faced with a possible death sentence."

"Why do you think that is?"

"I don't know." I ponder the question. "It seems so wild that we've made it this far. And this isn't the first time we've been in danger, viral or otherwise. Also, I think I have survivor's guilt. That we're alive when everyone else died is so unfair."

"Don't say that. Nothing about the virus was fair," he says. "Anyway…fair and unfair are from another world. They don't matter anymore."

"On the off chance we don't die of the virus in the next few days, we have to figure out how to parent this small person."

"Don't remind me."

"You know, you're doing great with her so far," I say. "I think patient, calm, and steady are exactly what she needs right now."

He grunts.

"How do you feel about having kids?" I ask. "Just out of interest?"

He sighs. "You mean back before fate forced the choice on me?"

"Mm."

"I don't know…maybe. What about you?"

"About the same." I give him side-eye. "I was half expecting you to give me some bullshit about the world needing us to help repopulate. To breed for the good of humankind or some such."

"I would if I thought it'd work. Don't think too highly of me."

I laugh softly. "No fear of that."

"The motorcycle won't fit the three of us. Assuming we're still alive tomorrow, I'll start looking for a vehicle. Something older without a lot of electronics. So you might as well get the mugs if you want them."

"You know much about engines?"

"Hopefully enough to get us by."

"I know how to check the oil and water and tire pressure, but that's about it."

"Something tells me we're going to be learning a variety of new skills in the next few years," he says. "That's if we survive tonight and tomorrow."

"Yeah."

He picks up the small CB radio and turns the dial, searching through the static for signs of life. Keeping the volume low, of course. Neither of us wants to wake Sophie. The first thing we hear is "It's the End of the World as We Know It" by R.E.M.

"Last night they were playing 'The Man Comes Around' by Johnny Cash," he says.

We wait for the next song, and it's "1999" by Prince. Whoever is broadcasting has a theme happening. I, for one, salute them. Bonus points for the gallows humor.

"I think I lack the energy to panic," I say. "Like I know I should be melting down at the idea of having the virus and dying, but I just can't be bothered. It seems like a step beyond where we're at right now."

"It was a hell of a day."

"You got shot. That was exciting."

He grunts.

"Imagine the amount of likes and comments we'd get on social media for surviving a day like today," I say. "What a waste."

"Your mind fascinates me."

I smile. "Don't misunderstand me. I am well aware that social media was a monster slowly eating itself from the inside out."

"And yet you took part in it."

"Of course I did. Don't act so high and mighty. Like you were too cool to be part of the online community of the time. Above the plebeian marketplace of memes and ideas."

"Would you friend me if it still existed?"

"Fuck no." I laugh softly. "Are you kidding me? You kidnapped me, dude."

He grins for like a millisecond. It's a flash of a thing.

"Where do you think we go after we die?"

Without a word, he rolls his head once more to the side to stare at me. And then stare at me some more.

"What?" I ask.

"You really want to talk about religion and shit right now?"

"Look who's grumpy when he gets shot. Take a painkiller and relax already."

The corner of his mouth twitches. It's so close to being a smile. "I want to be awake."

"We're doing guard duty?"

"I am," he says. "Yes. Just to be safe."

"Why don't I go first while you get some sleep? You lost blood today."

"Thanks," he says. "But as you said, I haven't taught you how to shoot yet."

"We spent an hour waiting and watching. That was me learning how to keep a lookout for any suspicious activity. My lungs and feet work just fine. I can shout or come wake you if I see something or get nervous."

He hesitates so hard.

I rise from the lounge. "Get some sleep and stop being such a big baby. I'll make a cup of coffee and go stand near the front door to keep lookout."

"Keep the lights off. You need your night eyes. Make sure you listen as well. And wake me in a couple of hours."

I am probably not going to wake him for at least twice that, so yeah. It's not a lie if you just don't answer.

"And thank you."

CHAPTER EIGHT

WEDNESDAY

SUNLIGHT AND SOFT VOICES WAKE ME. SOPHIE IS reading aloud from a book about wabi-sabi. The Japanese philosophy of finding value in broken or imperfect things. Dean nods and makes occasional comments, such as "interesting" and "okay." Guess literature choices are limited in the home goods store. But she is loving the attention, and he seems happy to be giving it. Which is nice.

No one is coughing or sneezing. Thank fuck. You would have thought our luck would be running out by now. However, here we are, still alive. Religion isn't my thing, though I'm starting to think someone is on our side. We might just live long enough for us to figure out how to raise a tween together, build a community, and become friends. Stranger things have happened.

I mean, we're still alive. Nothing is impossible.

Dean goes exploring and finds an old white Ford Ranger. It's been somebody's pride and joy. I doubt the truck has been driven on a day outside of Sunday in years. Lifted four inches and polished to within an inch of its life. The interior is immaculate, with *The Rise and Fall of Ziggy Stardust and the Spiders from Mars* by David Bowie in the tape deck. Sophie is less than impressed with the choice of music.

We fill a bag at her house with photos, clothes, and a few other favorite items. I asked her if she'd like her mom to be buried in the garden. But she seemed more upset about the idea of her mother being disturbed or removed from the bedroom. Should she change her mind in the future, we can always plan a trip and come back to see to her wishes.

Then we head south toward Wolf Creek.

I offer to drive so Dean can rest his arm, but he's too much of a control freak to give over the wheel. What a surprise. We have to turn around and find different routes a few times due to traffic pileups and such. Cows on the road also slow us down. Sophie and I take the opportunity to say moo to them, but Dean declines to join the conversation.

Taking a direct route on the highway would have gotten us there in half a day. Assuming there were no overturned semitrailers or crashed planes or whatever. The world went down in messy and chaotic ways. But I am reasonably certain we're doing the journey in a slow and indirect manner to avoid other people, and to make sure we're not being followed. There have to be some humans left out there who aren't assholes. Finding them will be the trick.

There used to be so many people wandering around taking up space. Protecting your peace, carving out your corner of the world, was the trick. It was easy to see people as passersby or competitors. But now with far fewer people, we need some who might be prospective friends or found family.

Rebuilding the world will take a whole lot more than us.

One thing we learn on our journey—children have no chill. Just none. Being contained in the truck all day drives Sophie wild. In the afternoon, we stop at a small swimming hole fed by a natural spring and set up camp for the night. It's a good chance for us all to get clean again. Sophie's long hair takes some work; then she lives her best life splashing about mermaid style. She jumps and splashes and screams her lungs out. Children really know how to live and they don't mind doing it loud.

Dean stands guard while we're in the water. The campground is reasonably secluded and back from the road. But he still digs a hole for our fire to hide some of the light.

We haven't seen anyone else all day. That is, no one alive. There have been bodies in vehicles and some outside of houses in various states of decay. Like they went looking for help at the end. Or maybe they just didn't want to die alone. What we *did* see is a pack of dogs gathered around something out front of a barn. I didn't want to know what they were eating.

I tried to distract Sophie from the sight. But the world is full of dead bodies now. It's not something I have a hope in hell of protecting her from. She got quiet after the first few, then just sort of started ignoring them. I don't know if it's a healthy attitude. So damn much I don't know when it comes to children.

For dinner, she ate more of the freeze-dried mac and cheese and then cried herself to sleep while I rubbed her back again. Of course, she misses her mom. I miss mine. Surviving the end times is sort of like falling down the rabbit hole. It takes time to find your footing.

Dean went for his dip in the dark while I watched for lights or movement or anything. And I sit with my back to the swimming hole. What the man looks like naked is none of my business. He can skinny-dip in peace, as far as I am concerned. Parade around naked for all I care. Though he's probably wearing his underwear, the same as me. Dark boxer briefs would be my guess.

Not that I'm wondering about his underthings, dripping wet and clinging to his body, because how weird would that be?

THURSDAY

"What the fuck?"

"Astrid," Dean chides me. The hypocrisy of him being the language morality police is not lost on me.

"Sorry." I open the passenger-side door to the truck and climb out. "Sophie, can you just wait here for a couple of minutes, please? Let us take a look around and make sure this is safe?"

"You won't go far?" asks the girl.

I give her a reassuring smile. "I'll stay where you can see me, okay?"

She nods and returns her attention to the book in her hands. I love how she's a reader.

Wolf Creek is situated between a waterway and some mountains. We passed a "Population: Five Hundred and Eighteen" sign a short distance ago. The grass is green and the mountain air is fresh. Apples and grapes are grown in the area. We just need to find out what else.

Our first attempt to enter the town turned out to be a bust, due to the small bridge leading to it having been blown up. There was nothing left but burnt wood and twisted metal. Guess we should have guessed then that something was going on.

Now the one remaining road into town is blockaded. Just before the gas station, mechanic, and bait shop, there's a motley collection of vehicles. With a tank and some other military types on one side and a school bus, a bunch of tractors, and a variety of trucks on the other.

And there are bodies. So many bodies. The town's population has definitely dropped. Given the guns lying around, it wasn't all due to the virus, either. Some sort of standoff happened here.

"Looks like they tried to force an evacuation," says Dean. "The townsfolk fought back."

"Why force them to evacuate? Where were they going to take them? What purpose would it've served?"

He just shakes his head. None of it makes sense.

How someone would kill for control when the world was already going down the tube. The way in which they were willing to put more people in danger for some pointless government fuckery. There are some things I will never understand, and I am honestly okay with that.

Beyond this mess are the nine neat blocks that make up the bulk of the town. They're laid out three by three, with offshoots leading to grocery and hardware stores, a small elementary school, and such.

Apart from the overgrown grass and bodies lying in the street, it could be an ordinary day here. Sun shining and flags flying. Bugs and birds are the only noise, however. The town square, with its old courthouse and cool stores, is as quiet as can be. We watch carefully for any signs of life, but there's seemingly nothing.

"Take this." Dean hands me a pistol. "The safety's off. You just point and shoot."

"You're going to check out the town?"

"Yeah," he says. "Keys to the truck are in the ignition. Don't hesitate to leave if you think it's unsafe."

"You'll find us?"

"Yeah." And it's a promise, not a threat. Another gun appears in his hands like magic. He jogs toward the town, the pose and awareness both broadcasting bad guy. Life was easier and simpler when I thought he was awful. But the truth is a more complicated thing.

I climb back in the truck and wait with Sophie for his return.

"If you had a dragon, would it be blue or green?" she asks.

"Good question. Those are the only two colors they have in your book?"

"So far."

I pretend to think it over. But I am a basic bitch at heart. "Blue."

"Yeah. Me too."

"Though green is also a great color."

"Mm."

She's so small. I know humans have to grow up and everything, but it's kind of terrifying being responsible for a whole other person all of a sudden. What if she gets a scratch and I don't notice and her head falls off or something? This is an extreme example to be sure; however, the fear is real.

"You know you can talk to me about anything, right?" I say.

"We could talk about friends you had at school or things you used to do at home, or anything really."

She blinks big eyes at me. "I just did talk to you."

"Yeah. Cool."

The child gives me a look of such dubiousness. Never before have my inadequacies been so eloquently expressed without words. I am doing amazing at this parenting thing. Just ask me.

Dean doesn't return for half an hour or so. And when he does, there's a light sheen of sweat on his skin. His running around searching towns after he got shot yesterday is perhaps not the best idea. But suggesting he take it easy would be a waste of time. The man thinks he's made of steel.

"What do you think?" I ask, handing him a water bottle.

He downs a mouthful and then says, "I think you're not the only one who wants this place."

"Leon and I got here Tuesday from Boise," says Natalia, and her husband gives her hand an affectionate squeeze. The way they act like newlyweds is sweet. Lots of affectionate looks and handholding. It's what I imagine love would be. And the size of the rock on her finger doesn't hurt none. "My first husband brought me here once on a fishing trip. I thought it might be a nice quiet corner of the world to see out our days in."

They're seated on the porch of the midcentury stone house they've settled into, while Dean and I stand a cautious distance away on the grass. None of us seem sick. No signs of fever or congestion or coughing. But it won't hurt to be careful and take things slow.

The house sits a block up from the town square and has

azaleas blooming by the front steps. Both Natalia and Leon are in their seventies, at a guess. He's a retired police detective, and she worked as a bookkeeper. Her long braid is silver and the same goes for his short afro and beard. Leon has a shotgun within reach and isn't hiding it. Which probably balances out whatever's on Dean.

"How did you get that bruise on your face?" asks Natalia.

"It came care of some not-so-nice people we encountered out on the road the other day," I answer. "Dean dealt with them. They won't be bothering anyone again."

Natalia nods. "Good."

"I could do without any more company," announces Leon. "But I suppose to stay here, we're going to need help disposing of the bodies. And no doubt other jobs will arise."

Dean nods. "Be happy to help, sir."

"You look big enough to be useful. Let me guess…Marine?"

"That's right."

"Knew there was a reason I didn't shoot you on sight," says Leon pleasantly.

Natalia watches Sophie do cartwheels on the grass with a smile. "How did you all survive?"

Dean keeps his mouth closed. But a muscle shifts in his jaw. Yeah. Telling people he kidnapped and caged me probably isn't the best idea. Not at the start. Not if we all want to stay. And what I do know about Dean for sure is that he would die for Sophie and me. Which is damn useful in an apocalypse.

"We were neighbors," I say. "Dean had a friend in government circles who gave him warning last week. He told me I'd probably die horribly if I didn't shelter in place with him. Then Sophie found us when we stopped in her town on Tuesday."

And it's all sort of the truth. Sort of. Just leaving out the little fact that I was in a cage when he told me he was saving my life.

"She was alone?" asks Natalia.

I nod.

Leon sighs. "Poor child."

"How about you two?" I ask.

"I didn't even know it was happening," says Leon. "Imagine my shock when I go to make my usual once-a-month grocery trip into town and find everyone has died."

"Apart from me." Natalia's smile is hesitant. "He found me sipping warm sweet tea outside an ice-cream shop. I didn't know what to do with myself. My daughter and her husband and all their three children caught the virus and died. Those poor sweet babies. I tended to all of them, but never had so much as a sniffle."

My eyebrows reach for the sky. "You mean you're immune? But you didn't pass it on to Leon, so…"

"So, no Typhoid Mary," says Dean. "That is welcome news."

"I wasn't sure who I should tell," says Natalia. "If my blood could be used for a cure or what. But by the time I tried to call the government and the hospitals, there was no one left alive to answer. It all happened so quickly. My daughter died first, and I couldn't…I couldn't just…"

"Don't upset yourself. You took care of your own and did your best," says Leon, giving her hand another squeeze.

"And you can't have been the only one," adds Dean.

"Do you think so?" asks Natalia.

Dean turns to me and asks, "What did you say? Population of over three hundred million?"

"That's right," I say.

"There's no way you were the only one, ma'am. They'd have found others and started doing testing. I think the virus just moved too damn fast for them to beat."

This kindness earns us our welcome here as much as anything. Because Leon frowns heavily and says, "Look for the houses with a ribbon tied around the front door handle. They don't have any dead bodies inside. Best to choose from one of them for your family."

Dean wants a sensible brick house on the far side of town. But he loses the vote, two against one, to Sophie and me. Of course, we fall for a charming hundred-year-old wooden house situated a block behind Natalia and Leon. It's painted blue and has a fireplace, butcherblock countertops, a clawfoot tub, and the necessary three bedrooms. There's even a vegetable patch primed for spring planting out back. Solar has been installed on the roof, but there's something wrong with the battery. Hopefully Dean can figure out the problem.

I think Sophie wants the house solely for the big old tree in the backyard with a tire swing. And fair enough.

As for me...this isn't the sort of place I could have ever hoped to afford. It's even situated on a large corner block with a view down to the creek. Not that property lines particularly matter now. But there's grass and trees and room for us to breathe. To plant more garden beds. Outside is a firepit and a shed with tools and hunting gear. Which makes sense, given the deer's head hanging on the living room wall. There's also a back porch with a barbeque and comfy chairs.

And as promised, there are no bodies in this house. No

smell to deal with outside of the rotting food in the fridge and freezer.

"Fine," says Dean. "You two get to choose this place. But I'm keeping the tank."

He's relaxing in one of the dark brown leather armchairs in the living room while I make a fire. Tonight is cool enough to warrant it. And smoke from a chimney at night doesn't stand out in the same way as it does during the day. There might still be buildings on fire in the cities, but we don't want to risk bringing attention to ourselves. Meeting new people needs to be done much more carefully with Sophie in the mix.

I wrinkle my nose in confusion. "The tank at the blockade?"

"Yes. One of the Joint Light Tactical Vehicles, too."

"Okay."

Sophie is fast asleep and sprawled across the matching brown leather couch. All of the cartwheels and handstands and inspecting houses took it out of her. There's a large navy-and-cream rug on the floor, cushions and throws in the same colors, and chunky antique wooden furniture. Whoever decorated the house had taste. It's a nice balance of style and comfort.

Sophie and I chose a photo of the family who used to own the house to leave hanging in the hallway. The rest of their photos are going into storage. We want to be respectful, but it's our place now. She also chose some pictures of her mom for her room and on the mantel. And when I am ready, I'll hang photos of my family too.

"It's a week today since this started," I say. "Happy anniversary."

"You don't seem to want to kill me quite as much as you used to."

"Eh."

"That's all you've got to say?"

I shrug and feed another twig to the fire. This is so soothing. Some part of me must be a pyromaniac. And I don't question why I'm content to share a house with my jailer or hang out with him. There has to come a time when his rights outweigh his wrongs. Or when his reasons for doing fucked-up things take precedence. I don't know. Nothing else in this new world makes sense. My thoughts and feelings for him aren't likely to be any different. He's going to help me keep Sophie safe, and that's the priority. For now, this is how things are and it feels right.

"Would she be better off with Natalia and Leon?" I ask, searching for another subject to worry over. Seems to be the night for it.

"Why would you think that?"

"They're older, wiser…Natalia has raised children and knows what she's doing."

He watches me in silence for a moment.

"What?"

"I am trying to figure out what you want me to say," he says. "What you want to hear."

"How about you just share your honest thoughts and feelings on the subject with me?"

The man sighs. "Okay. They're older, wiser, and Natalia

has raised children and does know what she's doing. But Soph chose you—"

"I was the first female that came along."

"She seems happy with us," he says. "It's only been a day or so. But she's eating and smiling and talking and doing all of the things she should be."

"She's also crying herself to sleep."

"Of course she is. Everyone she knew is dead. Where is this coming from?"

"I don't know."

"Neither of us were expecting to become guardians to a nine-year-old. Do you really not want…" And he doesn't finish the sentence. He doesn't need to. "Or are you worried we're going to mess things up?"

"The second one."

"Are you worried *I'm* going to mess things up?" he asks. "I'd understand if you are."

"No. As strange as it seems, I do trust you on this. I know you're on our side."

"I think that's what Soph thinks about you. She's knows you're on her side." He narrows his gaze on me. "I don't know, Astrid. I kidnapped someone for the first time last week. Not sure I should be giving advice on anything. Certainly nothing as important as she is."

"She *is* so important." I stare at the sleeping child. So angelic. "What if we just keep trying to do our best for now?"

"Sounds good to me."

"It's agreed, then. Good meeting."

"Right." He frowns and shakes his head. "Do you just like beating yourself up with ideas now and then or what?"

"I needed to be sure we were doing the right thing for her out of the options available to us."

"Guess it's good that you care," he says. "That you're trying to put her first. We need to be careful with anyone new coming in. Make sure they don't hurt her. She's been through enough."

"Yeah. Gun lessons starting tomorrow?"

"Tomorrow." He nods. "I can't wait to see what you're like when you're armed."

CHAPTER NINE

FRIDAY

"**F**RONT SIGHT, EJECTION PORT, SLIDE, AND REAR SIGHT." Dean points out each part of the weapon. "Safety lever and magazine release."

Sophie is wearing headphones and sitting in the front yard of a house where we can still see her. We decided to hold firearm classes after breakfast and water duties were done. Water duties involve hauling buckets of water from the creek to the house to be used in a variety of ways. To fill the toilet cistern and to wash with and such. My arms are going to be so toned.

Modern society made things so easy. Running water, electricity, disposal of trash…so many daily conveniences are gone. I will never understand people who used to dress up and pretend they were living in the past. This shit is intense. Though there is a beauty to the peace and quiet of all of this. A sort of simplicity to living this way, with no social media or streaming, or other distractions.

At any rate, here we are by the ruins of the bridge. Just a

few blocks away from our new home. I don't recognize my life anymore. I barely recognize me with a gun in my hand.

The braided hair, black tee, blue jeans, and hiking boots aren't wildly different from the old days. Which were only like a week or so ago. But the aching back from lugging buckets of water, with a child sitting nearby to worry over, and about to learn how to fire a gun kind of blows my mind.

"General warning," he says, bringing my attention back to the task at hand. "Don't draw it unless you're willing to use it, Astrid. Guns almost always escalate a situation."

"Understood."

"That being said, we both know how dangerous things can be now. If you need to protect yourself or Sophie, please don't hesitate."

I just nod. We're standing much closer together than normal. As if we're trading secrets. And being close to him isn't a big deal after all those days of being mooshed up against him on the motorcycle. No idea why I even noticed.

"Okay. Your grip when you hold it is going to be firm but not too tight," he says, handing me the weapon. "One hand holds the gun and the other supports it. Arms extended and feet shoulder width apart. But you're not going to lock your elbows or your knees."

"I hate guns."

"You wouldn't believe the shit I heard it saying about *you* earlier. Some of it was downright mean and petty. I was surprised."

"Very funny."

He grins. It's there and gone in an instant. And it does *not* make my belly tumble and turn. I just have gas or something.

"When you fire, it's a gentle squeeze," he says. "Don't jerk the trigger. You're going to shoot when you're breathing out. Keep it nice and calm and easy."

I arrange my body as told and try to calm myself. His hands cover mine, making incremental changes to their position. Straightening my shoulders some and nudging my foot in a few inches. And it's no big deal, the way he's touching me. Purely professional for the sake of what we're doing. But the warmth of his skin on mine lingers for some reason.

There are so many pine trees in the area and they smell beautiful out in the fresh morning air. For sure it's the flora getting me high.

What is wrong with me today? I wonder if I'm ovulating. It would explain things. Hormones are the worst.

"You okay?" he asks.

"Yeah. Yep."

The mess of tangled metal on the other side of the creek will do as a target. I concentrate on the sights and squeeze off a round. It makes a noise as it hits something. Of course, when your target is something the size of half a bridge, hitting the damn thing can't be too hard.

Dean nods. "Good work. Go again."

"I want to help you and Leon bury bodies today. It doesn't seem fair, that particular job falling on just you two."

He casts a look toward Soph over his shoulder. Checking she's still there and okay. "I appreciate you wanting to help. Natalia and Leon seem like good people. But we haven't even known them a whole day. One of us needs to be with Sophie."

I frown. "And we don't want her around any more dead bodies than strictly necessary."

"No, we don't. I'm bigger and stronger and can get the job done fastest out of the two of us, okay?"

"Okay. I'll clean out the fridge and freezer and sort out the rest of the house. Get rid of anything that's rotting and make some room for us. Also, we've got food for the next few days, but I want to see what's at the grocery store. Figure out if we need to go looking in the houses or think of making a trip farther afield."

"We should start making a list of stuff we're going to need. Solar panels and seeds and so on."

I nod and pick a point on the bridge, then aim and fire once again. There's no satisfying ping from hitting metal this time. But never mind.

"You don't hate the place," I say, and it's half question, half statement.

"I don't hate the place," he confirms. Though I can hear the silent *but*. "It's going to take a lot of work."

SATURDAY

"Oh no," I say with mock sadness. "The broccoli has gone bad. Those cabbages aren't looking so good either. Whatever will we do?"

Sophie barely reacts. Just keeps on bouncing the tennis ball she found out on the street. Guess she was due some down days with all she's been through. Grief has a habit of sneaking up on you and slapping you sideways when you least expect it. And she lost everyone and everything on top of the trauma of surviving on her own for several days. She had to have been terrified.

I wonder if she waited until we'd stopped somewhere to be

sad. Like she needed some safety and space to wade through those emotions. I don't know. But trying to get her to talk about it has not been successful so far. All I can do is wait and be here for her.

For someone who wasn't even certain she wanted children, Sophie sure does have me experiencing big feelings. I'm just thankful she found us in the drugstore. The idea of her out there on her own is horrible. At any rate, she's here and she's basically okay, and we're going to keep her that way.

Today we're in the market on the edge of town. Natalia's arthritis is acting up, so she's staying close to home. Soph and I are on our own with the grocery sorting. Dean disposed of the bodies of two people with shotguns guarding the front of the store, and another one from the back office. They all seem to have died of the virus while defending the place from looters. And they also seem to have succeeded. Not even the liquor store next door was touched.

Canned chili, soups, and stews are low in stock, along with instant mashed potato. Same goes for tissues, toilet paper, and cold and flu remedies. The sort of items you'd expect to have been popular during a pandemic.

Happily, though, the store isn't trashed and there's still plenty here for us to work with for the time being. How much of the canned food that's missing is still sitting in people's houses is another question. It's definitely worth looking for. Given how fast the virus worked, some people would have died before getting through their supplies.

Wolf Creek is slowly starting to come together. Leon and Dean used one of the tractors from the blockade to dig a mass grave beside the road into town yesterday. They're making good progress relocating the few hundred bodies needing to be laid to rest. Perhaps in time we can turn the area into a memorial garden. It would be good to do something to remember the people who were here before us.

The tank and one of the other military type vehicles that were facing off against the blockade are now parked on the street outside our house. Dean is living the dream. Watching him figure out how to steer the tank was entertaining. All of the stopping, starting, and swerving was reminiscent of a student driver figuring out a stick shift for the first time. Sophie laughed so hard she almost fell over. I can see the tank out my bedroom window, along with some charming trees.

Meanwhile, the school bus and other tractors have been moved to the side of the road heading into town for now.

We opted not to move all of the vehicles, however. They're useful, security-wise. Not for stopping people from gaining entrance. They can still enter on foot or if their vehicle is big enough to push a pair of sedans out of their way. But the small blockade should be useful, in theory, for slowing people down and perhaps giving us a chance to assess if they're friend or foe. And at least they'll make some noise and alert us to their presence.

Some of the fresh produce in the market can definitely be saved. Potatoes and pumpkins and corn and such. One week or so without electricity hasn't much affected the hardier vegetables. I start loading some into a cart, ready to push it out to the vehicle waiting in the parking lot.

Our deceased neighbors owned a nice midsize SUV, which is coming in handy for jobs around town. It feels sensible to stock the house with supplies. Say a week's worth, just in case we need to stay inside. And we need to restock the food in our backpacks in case we have to leave in a hurry. Which I really hope is not going to happen. But you never can tell these days.

"Can I go check out the candy aisle?" asks Sophie.

"Sure. Just don't leave the store or go out back without letting me know, okay? And don't eat a heap and make yourself sick," I say. "Once I sort out some vegetables, I'm going to head back to canned goods, then take this load out to the car. But definitely don't go somewhere else without letting me know. We still need to be security conscious."

I am not a helicopter-mom-slash-guardian type of person. I just sound a hell of a lot like one sometimes.

She nods and wanders off into the shadows of the store. Her footsteps and the bouncing of the ball are the only sounds.

It doesn't take long to fill the cart. On my way to the front doors, I call out, "I'm heading to the car, Soph."

Sunlight blinds me as I step outside. Clear blue skies all the way. The vehicle is pulled up right out front for convenience sake.

And standing beside it are five strangers in damp clothing.

Starting with a middle-aged Black woman with her hair in locs, then a lanky young white man in his twenties, a woman around my age with long red hair and botanical tattoos, a forty-or-so-year-old man with brown skin, and finally the most important person of all: an Asian-American girl around the same age as Sophie, with short hair and friendship bracelets on her wrists.

Their weapons are lying on the ground in front of them, sending a definite message. Without being asked, they've disarmed themselves. Small streams of water are running from their clothing.

They don't mean me any harm. I know this because the first thing their designated leader, the beautiful Black woman, says is, "We don't mean you any harm."

My walkie-talkie and weapon remain on my belt, just in case. Because I am wildly outnumbered here. Sophie needs to stay safely inside the store for a while. None of them seem sick, but I keep a careful distance. "You came in across the creek?"

"That's right," she answers. "We wanted to talk to you alone. See how receptive you were to new people. Your man carries a lot of weapons and seems quite handy with them."

"He can be intimidating."

"Then there's the tank parked outside your house."

"Would you believe me if I said that was more in the way of a garden ornament?" I ask. "How did you find us?"

"We were passing and heard the shooting at the bridge. Saw you with your daughter and knew we had to meet you," she says. "My name is Reema. And this is Charlie, Naomi, Avan, and Hazel."

"Astrid," I say with a cautious smile.

Avan has his arm around Hazel. There's no expression on her face. Just a sort of weariness it hurts to see in one so young. There's no way she's going back out on the road if I can help it. None.

"We're looking for a home," says Reema. "Somewhere safe for the child. One with others near her age, preferably. But we needed to know if you and the girl were here of your own voli-tion. That this is a safe place."

Dean would not like this. Me interviewing new people alone. But these people aren't giving me any bad vibes. "Where did you come from?"

"We escaped Bakersfield on Wednesday," says the redheaded woman, Naomi.

"Escaped?"

Reema nods. "There used to be eight of us. Soldiers were rounding up anyone they could find. Taking them to the military base outside the city."

"That must have seemed like a natural flow-on from martial law." I frown. "They weren't worried about the virus?"

"They had respirators," says Reema.

"What happened?"

"We heard the soldiers talking about how anyone who stepped out of line was being beaten." Reema stares hard at the horizon. "So, we picked our moment and…three didn't make it. But we got out of there. We got the child away from them."

"They were willing to hurt you rather than let you go?"

Reema nods again. "It's hard to trust people now. We know that better than anyone. All we want is a place where we can contribute in the way we're best suited for a fair share of resources and equal say in how things are done. As for what we have to offer…Avan is a paramedic."

And with those words, our population doubles.

"You're not my real mother," says Sophie with tears in her eyes before running into the house.

"Oof," I mumble.

Dean sighs. "They're not having a sleepover tonight. It's too soon. Let me talk to her. She's overtired. It's been a big day for everyone."

"Go for it."

No idea how people manage being single parents. Talk about superheroes. I am already slightly scared of the teenage years ahead of us.

Everyone else is gathered around the firepit in our backyard for the welcome party. We ate potatoes and corn baked in the fire, along with an assortment of canned foods. Soda and beer were cooled care of the creek. Things seem almost normal. Just a group of people hanging out. Naomi plays guitar while Leon and Avan trade first responder stories. Ones not too gruesome for the girls to hear.

Natalia took one look at Hazel and agreed on the new group staying. But it took some time to convince Leon and Dean. The lure of someone with medical training won out, however. And after half a day spent together, the two girls are firm friends. There's no way Dean could separate them now. Sophie would start a war.

The sky is full of stars and it's a beautiful show. Adirondack chairs, fancy cushions, and an assortment of throws are gathered around the firepit. Single-malt scotch and top-shelf silver tequila are being passed around. Leon smokes some fancy cigar. Life can be so bougie when money doesn't matter.

Seems Avan and Hazel were immune. The rest of the group managed to avoid catching the virus. The apocalypse really is the great leveler in a lot of ways. Reema was a partner in a law firm. Naomi a tattoo artist. And Charlie did road maintenance. Now we're all survivors.

Avan and Charlie sit together, holding hands. Like Leon and Natalia, they seem to have found love amidst the horror. Imagine experiencing beauty and euphoria in the midst of such terror and loss. None of them might have even met otherwise.

Life is such a strange thing. It really doesn't make sense on even the best of days.

"She yours?" asks Naomi, intercepting me halfway back to the fire pit. She's like a kick-ass Anne of Green Gables with her long red hair, botanical tattoos, and the knife on her hip. I want to be her when I grow up.

"Sophie? You could say she chose us."

"Did you have children before?"

I shake my head. "This is all new to me, can't you tell? How about you?"

"No, I didn't have any. But I think you're doing really well." She gives me a small smile. "Reema lost two sons. She mostly handles Hazel due to her experience with kids. I think they're helping to heal each other, you know?"

"Yeah."

Hazel is curled up, lying on a blanket with her head in Reema's lap. I really hope having this group join us works out. Having more people around feels right. We still need to get to know one another and feel safe around each other, though. They need to pick out a house to live in, and we need to work out how we all fit into this small community and how we move forward with our life here.

"And is *he* yours?" asks Naomi with a disarming smile.

"Huh?" It takes me a moment to work out what she's asking. Sophie isn't the only one who's overtired. Or maybe I just don't want to hear this particular question. "You mean Dean?"

"Yeah. Not to stick my nose in…but is it more of a friend thing or…" The woman actually blushes and looks away.

"You're interested in Dean?"

"He's an attractive guy who doesn't seem to be a criminal. They're kind of thin on the ground these days."

"No. He doesn't *seem* to be a criminal," I agree, with much awkwardness. "Um. I don't know what to say. It's complicated."

"Guess I'll just wait and see." Naomi heads back to the fire with a hint of a smile on her face. Which is fine. It's perfectly fine.

CHAPTER TEN

SATURDAY

DEAN STANDS BESIDE THE FRONT WINDOW, WATCHING the street outside. The same position he's been in for the last half hour. Ever since we finished hand washing in the laundry tub. No idea why I felt the need to do laundry at this hour of the night after the welcome party. Guess it was to expend some nervous energy.

I did the soaping and scrubbing; he handled wringing the clothes and hanging them out to dry on an airing rack we found. We even managed to behave like adults and not make handling each other's underwear too weird. And all of this happened while Sophie told us the top one hundred most interesting facts about her new best friend. When we finally got her to go to bed, she was out like a light. The sleepover wasn't mentioned again. I've been forgiven for now.

"I don't like it," he says, for not the first time. "Think about it…why'd they pick a house a block away from us? What are they hiding, huh?"

"You wanted us to live on the opposite side of town."

"That's beside the point."

"How about there aren't that many houses large enough for their group to comfortably stay together?"

He grunts.

"You thought they were okay after the welcome party. What changed?"

"I don't know. Maybe I'm just being paranoid."

I sit in the corner of the couch, thinking deep thoughts. "The more people we have, the safer we're going to be from predators like the ones they were talking about."

"Yeah," he says. "There is strength in numbers, and it makes us less vulnerable to ambush. But we need to be careful. Not everyone is going to be happy to have some sort of democracy with law and order."

"You're worried about a hostile takeover?"

He shrugs and checks the street again through the gap in the curtains.

"It's not like there's going to be a grab on resources anytime soon. Everything is still out there. The only thing we're short on these days is people," I say. "Wait. Are you worried they could have been followed by those assholes from Bakersfield? Is that what this is about?"

"It's one possibility."

"Hmm. Today was a good day," I say. "Making new friends, hanging out around the fire…it was nice. It doesn't seem right, does it? To enjoy life when so many other people died? I know it's just more survivor's guilt, but it's hard to ignore sometimes."

"What would your mom want you to do?"

"To go on living my life to the best of my abilities."

He nods. "I better go. I've got the first watch. Leon is taking second. We're going to keep an eye out for at least a night or two."

"I can take third watch. Cut down on the time you're both out there."

"Not until you've had a few more firearm lessons. Keep the walkie-talkie by your bed just in case, okay?" His gaze is as serious as can be. "If I see a few people, you grab Soph and get in a cupboard. More than that and you both hide down by the creek, wait for me, and we leave town."

"I know the plan."

"Firearms are stored in the locked cupboard out in the shed and the secure boxes in my wardrobe and on the top shelf of the pantry, okay?" he says.

"I talked to Sophie about not touching any guns. But we need to keep doing that regularly. Things she should and shouldn't pick up. As previously mentioned, everything's just out there lying around, ready and waiting."

"Agreed." His expression is still serious as he says, "Naomi seems to know her shit. Said her dad was a survivalist. Used to take her hunting and made sure she knew how to defend herself."

"Okay."

"He was the one who called and told her to isolate early on."

My smile feels off for some reason. Like it isn't sitting right on my face. So strange. "Sounds like you two had a good chat."

"She's been teaching Reema and Charlie some stuff. They're going to start joining us at morning lessons," says Dean. "Not with guns. I don't want them near you with firearms until we know them better. But learning self-defense from a woman might be useful for you."

"Right."

"They're all happy to help with the dead bodies and sorting out supplies. Avan wants to focus on putting together a decent medical setup. Just in case."

"That makes sense."

"Yeah." He nods. "Naomi said—"

"For someone who doesn't trust them, you sure seem to like them. Or some of them, at least."

He freezes and his forehead fills with furrows. "What's wrong?"

"Nothing."

He studies my face like I'm a puzzle to be figured out. "Talk to me."

"Really, it's fine." I give him the fakest smile in all of time and space. But it doesn't hold and he doesn't seem the least bit convinced.

This sucks. The confusion. The tangle of emotions in my head and my heart. Logically, Dean as an interest of my like or love is wrong and bad. However, all of the thoughts and feelings inside of me are so fucking complicated.

"Sit down a minute," I say.

"You want me to sit down?"

"Yes. Next to me." I contain myself to one end of the leather couch. "Here."

The glance he gives me is wild. Rattlesnakes have been looked at with less caution. Scorpions have been cozied up to with more warmth. "What's going on, Astrid?"

"There's something I need to know."

He just waits.

No point in half-assing this. For the purposes of scientific research, it must be done.

I climb onto his lap so that our chests are facing each other and I'm straddling him. And his expression is everything, with his mouth open slightly and his eyes as wide as can be. His hands immediately grip my thighs good and tight. Like he's scared I'm going to try to get away.

"Don't move," I say.

He frowns. It's truly his favorite face.

This position puts me a little above him in stature. He feels good and solid beneath me. And I can do whatever I want and touch him how I like. Talk about a power trip. It's nice to be the one calling the shots for a change. His gaze takes in my face, my neck, and my chest. There's a tension to him. An odd sort of wired energy.

I brush my fingers through his thick hair, pushing it back from his face. Then I trace the pads of my fingers over those oh-so-familiar furrows on his brow and the line of his jawbone.

He holds himself perfectly still beneath my exploration, letting me do as I please. Given how his shoulders are rising and falling, however, it takes considerable effort for him to remain still. To allow someone else to have control.

His skin is warm and the stubble on his jaw rough. There are hints of gray the same as the threads in his hair. He has lines near his eyes from squinting into the sun. Not so many bracing his mouth from smiling. Something I would very much like to change.

I press my face against his thick, strong neck. Damn, he smells good. Salt and pine and something just him. Hiding here feels safe. The world could fall and rise a hundred times and none of it would matter.

"Are you sniffing me?" he asks with interest.

"Shh. Don't ruin it."

"Sorry."

Shit. Such bad news. I like this and I want him. It's a definite. Things are happening in both my heart and pants regions. I was really hoping to avoid same but there's no denying it. And he's growing hard against me from just this much contact.

"You like this, don't you?" he asks. "Being in control."

"Maybe."

"Hmm."

I rock against him, and we both catch our breath. The way his eyes dilate is a thing of beauty.

"Don't know if I ever told you, but I used to read a lot of romance," I whisper in his ear. "Monster fucking was my thing."

The way he groans. Causing him pain like this is such a pleasure. And if it's wrong to giggle at someone's discomfort then so be it. I am wrong.

"You're going to talk yourself out of this, aren't you?" he asks in the calmest of tones.

"That's between me and my brain."

"Pity."

I snort and climb off of him. This needs to get shut down before it goes too far. "Go walk in the cold night air and think chaste thoughts, Dean."

"Yeah. I'll do that." He shoves a hand through his hair. "Let's experiment with the touching again soon. In fact, I think it should be a regular activity from now on. Every night, once Soph's gone to sleep."

"I'll think about it."

He cocks his head. "That's not a no."

And out the door he goes with a smile on his face.

SUNDAY

"I was stuck at home with some nasty bug," Reema tells me. "How's that for irony?"

We're going through the empty houses one by one. Leon and Dean had to break into the bulk of them. Sometimes through a window, so we're careful of broken glass. Weapons and ammunition, medications, and any foods not requiring refrigeration are top of the list of items we're after. Wandering around in people's homes like this feels so strange.

Sophie and Hazel are hanging out on the front porch while we search inside. They were keen to come inside and help. But given that we found a semiautomatic sitting on a coffee table at the last place, it's best if they wait outside until we're sure the spaces are safe. And the walkie-talkie is again attached to my belt in case of emergencies.

"Came down with it on the Friday," says Reema. "I told my boys, don't come over, you don't want to risk getting it. Then this new virus was spreading, and they were so worried about me catching it since my immune system had already taken a beating. I worked from home for a few days just to pacify them. But by then…"

"I'm so sorry. That sounds trite, doesn't it?"

"There isn't one of us who hasn't lost someone. And most of us have lost everything."

Of course, she's right. But to lose your children…I can't imagine the sort of pain she's carrying. The same goes for Natalia. Sophie has been with me for a few days, and I already feel more for her than I could have imagined.

Reema admires a cabinet full of blue and white porcelain in the living room. "Someone liked pretty things."

It's a delicate balance between being respectful and getting the job done. These houses are full of stories. Photos of family and friends and the remnants of everyday life. I find this fascinating in a way, poking around in people's homes. Guess I'm curious by nature. Nosy is another word for it, and not an incorrect one either.

Reema checks out the pine cupboards and cream tile counters in the kitchen. "This hasn't been changed since the eighties."

"The lace curtains are something."

"They're dreadful. Be honest. My auntie had ones just the same."

I laugh and head for the pantry. "We have canned chili and clam chowder, and a bag of onions. Quite a few jars of pickles and olives, too. I am calling this a win."

"Dirty martinis are back on the menu. That's *definitely* a win. Let's see what the medicine cabinet has in store for us. Some more amoxycillin would be good."

We're collecting any and all medicines. Avan will sort the useful from the not so much. He, Naomi, Charlie, and Dean are working on the dead body problem. It was identified as being the most immediate issue. Meanwhile, Leon is resting after taking the second watch during the night and Natalia is keeping an eye on the road into town.

There's a tidy selection of market bags just waiting for me to start packing groceries. Today's sore muscles come care of carrying jars and cans out to the car and hauling buckets of water from the creek to the house earlier. Not to forget learning how to throw a punch in this morning's self-defense class. Eyes, throat, and groin are now drilled into my head as prime attack spots.

Everything that mattered to me a month ago is gone now. All of my plans and priorities are dust. There was surviving the virus. Then there's sticking the landing through all of the changes of the aftermath. Not just the loss of friends and family, but having your life turned upside down. Food, water, safety, shelter, and companionship didn't used to take this much effort. I was also so much luckier than I ever understood.

The supplies we find are being split among the three houses at present. Once we are assured of a continuous supply of food for the next while, we can move on to other jobs. Like preparing and planting the gardens. For which we need to check out the local hardware store, where they will hopefully have some seeds and everything else we're going to need. It's on this afternoon's agenda. But sooner or later we're going to have to go farther afield in search of things like solar panels and a generator. And what I really want is more information on how to do all of these things.

In the meantime, I am not the least bit worried about Naomi working with Dean. It hasn't even crossed my mind once. He kidnapped *me*. Not her. And I cannot fucking believe I just said that to myself. Honestly. There better be a therapist still alive and willing to barter for services. Otherwise, me and my Stockholm syndrome are in serious trouble.

Me and him as a couple make no sense. My head knows this. But my heart and loins aren't listening. In any other situation, during any other time, this wouldn't even be an option. Of course you don't date the dude who kidnapped you. We are, however, talking about the end of the world. And the old rules do not apply.

Sad to say, it's a glass cookie jar that tips my emotions over the edge. It's nothing even to do with Dean. Nope. It isn't even anything to do with Sophie. She's perfectly fine. Out hanging on the porch with her new best friend.

But I see the glass cookie jar hidden at the back of the cabinet, and it's the exact same one my mom and dad had at their house. The *exact* same. There are even a couple of Girl Scout cookies left inside. It stops me dead. Getting sucker punched honestly hurt less.

I just lose it and start crying, which is ridiculous.

Dean joins me at the fire with a bottle of beer in hand. His hair is still damp from bathing in the creek. There's a masculine beauty to him that gets me every time. He sits on the blanket beside me with an easy smile, but he doesn't fool me. His sharp gaze moves over Sophie before doing the same for me. Just checking we're still in one piece and no one's hurt his girls.

And I don't stare at him like he's the stuffed toy my father gave me all those years ago. I don't need him to cuddle and comfort me. Everything is fine.

Tonight's dinner is being hosted by the town's newest members. The place they chose to move into is an elegant old three-story wooden house with a wraparound veranda. What used to be one of the bed-and-breakfasts in town, which explains the good amount of bedrooms.

Stones from the woods surround the new firepit constructed on the overgrown front lawn. Avan has made flatbread out of flour, oil, and water. My contribution was homemade hummus due to the surplus of canned garbanzo beans. It involved a whole lot of mashing with a fork; however, I love hummus, so it was well worth the effort. And Natalia spent the day fishing in the creek in view of the road into town. Figuring out food three times a day can be a chore without modern conveniences. But sitting around a fire with new friends is sublime.

"Talk to me," he says in a low voice.

"Hi, Dean. How was your day?"

"We got a lot more done with the extra hands." He takes a look at the people gathered around the fire. "They all seem okay."

"I wholeheartedly agree."

Sophie takes a quick break from mapping out constellations with Hazel—they're in one of the books they found at the library—long enough to remove one of the crystal bracelets on her wrist and slide it onto Dean's.

"This is for me?" he asks.

"Yes," she says.

"Thank you."

And then she's gone again and back with her friend. Seeing her smile is the best feeling. Hazel seems happier today too, which is great.

"We went shopping on the square this afternoon. They were in a boutique," I explain, inspecting his bracelet. "We both needed more jeans and tees. Only having one change was getting old. The girls loved trying on the coats in the vintage clothes store. She gave you the gray agate bracelet. I got turquoise."

"Are crystals meant to have special properties? What does gray agate mean?"

I steal a sip from his bottle of beer. "No idea."

"It probably means I am incredibly understanding now."

"Probably."

"So understanding, you'll just automatically tell me all about what upset you earlier without me even prompting. Because you know whatever happened, my response will be thoughtful and kind."

"Subtle."

"You like that?" He takes back the bottle of beer. "Reema mentioned you had a tough day."

I sigh. "It was just a moment. One of those *a whole lot of the people I love have died* kind of moments, you know?"

"Sorry you were feeling low."

"Thanks."

His dark brows draw down. "But not all of the people you love?"

"Don't do it, Dean. Don't go there."

The corner of his lips twitch in an almost smile. And I don't smile at his nonsense. Much. "Can we talk about it?" he asks, getting serious again.

"It was just…I saw something that reminded me and… missing them is part of being alive and still loving them, right?"

"Yeah. I guess so."

And there Naomi sits, playing guitar on the other side of the campfire. When she catches me watching her watching *him*, she gives me a wink. Ha. Good on her for owning what she wants. Having her help with the self-defense stuff in the morning lessons is already proving useful. I can't find it in me to resent or dislike her. Any jealousy on my part is my own problem.

"What are you grateful for today?" he asks me.

"Books. What about you?"

"Books are great. But I am going with ice-cold beer," he says, pausing to take another swig. "This isn't bad, but it's not like it was. I'm still savoring it, though. Because there's going to come a time in the not-too-distant future when there's no more beer. First the IPAs will go. Then the ordinary lagers. Then even the stouts will turn bad. That's when the end of the world will *really* start. And I don't know a damn thing about brewing or growing hops."

"We have a lot to learn."

"So much," he says. "I saw the library books when I stopped by the house. You're ready to get the garden going?"

"The sooner we start, the better."

"Look in any of the other stores on the square?" he asks.

"We didn't bother going into the art gallery, antiques store, or ice-cream parlor. But the homeware store and apothecary had candles, and the café had a good stock of coffee beans. Lots of alcohol in the wine bar and the inn. There was also a solid store of condiments, some canned food, and pasta and rice in the vegan restaurant."

"We haven't cleared the inn yet."

"The girls waited outside," I say. "It was fine. I think we've got a decent amount of food for now."

"We need to see what we can do about getting the power back on. In a couple of days, let's make that trip to the big hardware store out by the highway. Take a couple of trucks and start collecting the things we think we're going to need. Store them closer to home if nothing else. They'll have a wider range of seeds and stuff for you to choose from," he says. "You're basically competent with a gun now. It feels like the right time."

"Take Sophie with us or leave her here? I don't love the idea of her being out there. Not only is it dangerous, but I worry about her seeing things that might retraumatize her."

"See how trusting we're feeling when the day comes?"

"Okay," I say. "Did you really have to teach her how to whistle with her fingers?"

"What's wrong with that?"

"It's so loud and she does it in the house. My hearing is basically gone in one ear."

"I'll talk to her."

"Thank you," I say. "I don't want to be bad cop all the time. There needs to be an even division of labor when it comes to who's handing down the life-ruining decisions."

He cocks his head.

"What?"

"Just imagining you with handcuffs."

"Dream on." I watch him for a minute. He passes me the bottle of beer again, thinking it's what I want. "Things are going well, aren't they?"

"Yeah."

"So why are you frowning?"

Now he frowns even harder. "I don't know. You ever feel like things are going *too* well?"

"Such a pessimist."

"Maybe," he says. "Seemed like we were in shitty situations pretty regularly out on the road. I don't trust this quiet."

"How about we just enjoy tonight?"

He's quiet for a while. Then he says, "If I'm planning for disaster and ways for us to survive…that takes hope, right?"

"Yes. That takes hope."

"That's what I thought," he says with a smile.

CHAPTER ELEVEN

WEDNESDAY

WE USE A COUPLE OF PICKUP TRUCKS FOR THE TRIP. Charlie and Naomi in one, and Dean and me in the other. The tanks are full but there are containers of gas in the back, along with the siphons, of course. One day we're going to have to work out how best to access the reserve at the gas station in town. For now, however, there's plenty just sitting in cars waiting to be used. Extra food and ammunition have also been packed. Just in case.

The store is situated to the east of us on the edge of a much larger town. It's half an hour's drive on the highways. But we take the longer way on the back roads just to be safe. Sophie stays behind. She's more than happy to spend the day hanging out with Hazel. Reema is watching the girls. Natalia and Leon are fishing. And Avan is sorting medicine and medical equipment. He decided to set up a spare bedroom at the bed-and-breakfast as our hospital for now.

I spent the last two days building raised garden beds in our yard with cinder blocks. There was a surplus of them behind the hardware store. Given how reasonably lightweight and easy they were to work with, they won out over timber. I would have had to wait for help from someone else otherwise, and I was keen to get the garden happening.

Once the ground was broken and the grass and weeds were removed, the cinder blocks could be put into place. Then it was just a matter of stealing soil from here, there, and everywhere to build up the garden beds. Talk about spending quality time with a pick, spade, and wheelbarrow. Our local hardware had a few bags of fertilizer, and some people in the area had been composting.

Seed starter trays from the hardware are set up inside the house. Sophie and Hazel enjoyed helping with them. One of the books said it was the right time of year for pumpkins, cucumbers, and zucchini. Books on canning and pickling are going to be needed on the next trip to the library. There's so much to learn.

My grandmother would laugh if she could see me. She tried to get me interested in gardening when I was a child. We would grow strawberries, cucumbers, and tomatoes together in the summer. But it was never really my thing. Now it needs to be my thing if we want to eat fresh food. So I do my best to ignore the blisters and the aches and pains from all of the picking and shoveling.

However, today I am riding in a pickup truck wearing a pistol on my hip. You never quite know what the apocalypse will throw at you from one day to the next. My nerves are making an appearance. Guess I got used to being in town. Being out on the road again feels weirdly exposed. Like I have a target on me.

Though it's not my only concern. And I can't stop fidgeting with the cap on my water bottle or the seam on my tee.

"You carried me to bed last night," I say out of nowhere.

"You keep passing out early on the couch," he complains.

"I can't help that you're such scintillating company."

His smile is there and gone in an instant. Like he has to hide it or something. And it's downright unfair the way sunglasses increase his general hotness. "The garden's wearing you out. How are your hands?"

"I wore the gardening gloves yesterday. You were right—it was better."

"Can you say that again?" he asks. "The part about me being right…"

"No. And anyway, you shouldn't be carrying me around. It could hurt your arm."

"My arm is fine."

With the window down, the wind tears at my ponytail. We pass fields, forests, warehouses, and the occasional house. No sign of any people out there living their lives. It's a big, wide, empty world.

"Thought this might be a good chance to talk about how you've been avoiding being alone with me for the last few days," he says, keeping his steady gaze on the road.

"Is that why you vetoed Naomi riding with you? She wasn't happy."

Nothing from him, which is interesting.

"Didn't we just cover that I've been tired and crashing early?"

"Yeah," he says, easy as can be. "But it's more than that, isn't it? Being too busy to talk to me in the morning. Getting out of the house as soon as you can. You're not exactly subtle."

My mouth stays shut tight.

"The question is…are you desperate enough to throw yourself out of a moving vehicle to avoid having this conversation with me?"

"Very funny."

"Thanks," says the jerk with a smile. "Now we both know my experience with relationships is limited. But I've been giving this little problem between us some thought and I think I've got it figured out."

I just wait.

"My theory is that you got sort of intimate with me, and you liked it, and now you're not sure how you feel about things." The forehead furrows make an appearance. He's clearly having deep thoughts or big feelings or something. "Not sure if you're worried about us getting closer, and the possibility of losing someone else since all of your friends and family died. That's a lot of hurt to put on one heart. But it might also just be due to our complicated history."

"And by history, you mean last week or so." It's hard to know what to say. "My honest answer is, I don't know. Maybe. I need more time to think it through. Get comfortable with the idea maybe."

"Okay."

"You're letting it go that easy?" I ask in surprise.

He takes a deep breath. "Here's the thing…I have feelings for you."

"I assumed they existed in some part of you. But are we talking in the pants or the heart?"

"Both."

"So you want to fuck me, but you also want to cuddle me and listen to me speak nonsense."

"That honestly sounds like a perfect date to me."

I can't hold back the smile.

"But you're still making up your mind," he says. "You're attracted to me, but you're wary. I'm here when you're ready to talk about it."

"Thank you." Which makes it the perfect time for a change of topic. "How long are you going to keep doing the night watches?"

"Not sure."

"You haven't seen anything?"

"No. It's been quiet."

"That's good," I say. "But if you feel it needs to be an ongoing thing, then we all need to start doing our share."

He raises a brow. "You're thinking maybe it *should* be ongoing?"

"I haven't forgotten those assholes who were there when we had to leave your place and when we got stopped out on the road. Heard anything interesting on the CB radio lately?"

"Three different people have declared themselves President, and there's at least one king."

I raise my brows. "Aim high, that's what I always say."

"Yeah." He pauses. "And apparently, there's a group forming to the south of us."

"How close?"

"About an hour's drive away. They're inviting people to join them."

"That's not too close. Do they sound nice or not so much?"

"Hard to tell," he says with a frown. "What they're saying… it's not really enough to get a feel for the situation."

"But you don't trust them. Of course, you don't actually trust anyone, so that doesn't necessarily mean much."

"That's not true. I trust *you*."

This stops me. "You do?"

"Yes." And he sounds so certain. But he doesn't dwell on it. "Someone said the CDC in Atlanta is empty. Everyone there's dead."

"Disappointing but not exactly unexpected. Is the end-of-the-world station still playing songs?"

"Last night was Crowded House, 'Don't Dream It's Over'. I keep thinking they'll run out of songs, but no," he says. "They played one called 'Clarity' that I liked. It was about how it takes the end of the world for this guy to realize that all he really cares about is the girl."

Our eyes meet, and yeah. That's a big no comment from me.

"I want you to teach me what you're learning about gardening," he says. "We're going to need more than just you working on that side of food production in the future."

"Okay."

The parking lot of the behemoth store is mostly empty. Just a few cars here and there, along with some bodies rotting in the sun. Making your way through the world these days is like walking through a graveyard. Though it probably always was to some degree. Bodies were just usually buried before. Things are less neat and tidy now.

Dean parks the pickup alongside the front doors, ready to go in case of trouble. And Naomi and Charlie park alongside us. There's no sign of smashed glass or forced entry. We might be the first people to stop by here post-apocalypse wise.

There's a hill hiding the bulk of our view of the town to the west. Though we can see a thin line of smoke trailing up into the air. So there might be some people somewhere in the area. But everything seems quiet.

With a bolt cutter, Dean makes short work of the padlock and chains holding the front doors together. "I don't like it," he says. "This security doesn't look original or official. Maybe we're not the first ones who've checked out this place."

Inside, however, all is orderly and still reasonably well stocked from what we can see. And it's completely deserted.

"Let's go shopping," says Naomi, pushing a cart.

Dean gives me a nod before heading off in the opposite direction with Charlie.

The closest aisle has matches, fire starters, cooking grates, and heatproof gloves. Useful stuff for our firepit cooking. But every aisle seems to have something we could use. It isn't long before I'm jogging back to the front of the store for a second cart. Their range of seeds far exceeds the local hardware store's, and they have way more fertilizer on hand. Manure and peat moss apparently excite me now. Another change I didn't see coming.

"How are you and Dean doing?" asks Naomi with a friendly smile.

"None of your business."

"Fair enough." She grins. "But don't you think we'd make a cute couple?"

"You are such a shit-stirrer. Don't make me hit you. I'd probably miss."

The woman throws back her head and laughs her ass off.

Happy one of us finds the situation amusing. Though I *am* smiling, so…

We load up the back of one of the pickup trucks with our finds while Dean and Charlie do likewise with the other. Everything is happening in a swift and smooth fashion. We could be back in Wolf Creek in time for lunch at this rate. I even found some items in the craft section for Sophie and Hazel. Painting and mosaic sets and such. In this new world, the range of skills they'll need will be dramatically different from the old. But there's always room for art. There needs to be. Lose the beauty in your soul and you've got nothing.

Dean and Charlie are inside for one more load when a car pulls into the parking lot. It's a purple classic Camaro. And they waste no time getting over to us, wheels screeching and stereo blaring.

Both Naomi and I move our hands closer to our weapons. This is not good.

Two white men climb out of the car. One rests his arms on the roof of the vehicle, watching us from behind his dark sunglasses. And of course, he's got a shotgun.

The other wanders much closer than I like. He has short blond hair and is wearing a pair of pistols on his hips. He has one of those smiles you see on people who were told they're cute one time too many and decided to make it their entire personality.

Neither of them seems sick. But I'd still rather they kept their distance.

"What a lovely surprise," he says. "How are you doing, girls?"

Naomi and I just look at each other.

"Gosh, you two are pretty. But you're not friendly?" He

clutches at his heart like an idiot. "Well, that's a crying shame. You're going to hurt my feelings."

"Given a few billion people died," I say, "you're going to have to forgive us if we don't feel like flirting."

The man standing over by the car snorts but says nothing. He has shoulder-length dark hair and tattoos on one arm. There's a stillness to him I don't trust. It's like he's holding himself ready for something. And I would very much not like to get kidnapped or killed today. Dean and Charlie are safe inside for now, at least.

Sadly, my bad attitude doesn't dissuade creep number one. He doesn't climb back into his car and fuck off into the sunset. Instead, he steps closer, inspects the contents of the pickups, and asks, "Where'd you girls come from?"

Neither of us answers.

"Must be somewhere local to be wanting this sort of stuff and not just focusing on camping gear."

"Or the stores near us were picked over, so we decided to go for a drive," says Naomi.

"Why do I get the feeling you're lying to me?" The smile fades from his face as he comes closer. "Did you set up near one of the lakes in the west or are you from over by the coast? You can tell me..."

Both of our mouths stay shut. No way do we want these people knowing where we live.

Every woman has a story about a man like this. One who tried to corner and pressure and push her into doing what he wanted. Naomi and I back up a step and the creep follows. I don't think either of us wanted to get into a gunfight today. However, the odds for it are unfortunately on the rise.

"Maybe you came down from the north," he continues. "I heard a lot of those towns were burned to the ground. But who knows? How many more people are in your group? I'm guessing it's mostly women and children, or you'd have someone helping you lift all of this heavy stuff."

"Are you always this much of a patronizing ass?" asks Naomi. And honestly, it's a valid question.

He ignores the comment and takes another step closer. "Not going to tell me where you're from? No matter. We sure would love for you two to come see our place. Meet the man in charge of our community. You'd be a whole lot safer and well cared for with us. Why, we would just spoil you two lovely ladies rotten!"

"I don't think so," I say, braving it out.

But he's so close now. "Come for a visit. I think you'd be surprised how much you'd like it. And I'm not taking no for an answer."

"You're going to have to," says Naomi.

He gives our weapons a wary glance. Then he shakes his head sadly and says, "Such a shame. I was hoping we could come to some sort of agreement without any unpleasantness. But the thing is…I'm afraid you're going to have to put all of this back. Everything here has already been claimed by Porter."

"It's been claimed," I repeat in a dubious tone.

"That's right. He's claimed all of the resources in this area. You'd need to talk to him before we could allow you to take anything," he says. "I'm sure you understand."

"You'd be wrong about that."

This is the moment when everything goes to hell. I take another step back and my foot hits the curb behind us. My balance gets shot to shit and I'm falling.

The creep reaches out and grabs hold of me, keeping me on my feet. But of course he doesn't let me go. Instead, his hold on my arm tightens and he drags me closer for use as a human shield. Then he draws one of his pistols and points it at my head at point-blank range.

"Get your hands off her." Naomi reaches for her gun and aims it at him.

So much mutually assured destruction. Given what they want and how they think, I am not sure this was ever going to go any other way.

"You're not going to shoot me," says the creep in a condescending tone. "Doubt you could even hit me without hurting your friend. Come for a drive south with us, ladies. You're going to love your new home, I promise."

No is obviously not an acceptable answer for him. There's no way this is going to end well. Given that he doesn't want to give us an option about joining their community, I can just imagine what our life there would be like. No rights. No say in what happens to us.

When the firearm lessons first started, I wasn't sure if I could shoot someone. But I am not so worried about it anymore.

"Don't make me have to shoot you. That's what happened to those two over there." The creep nods to a couple of the bodies in the parking lot. "They tried to steal from Porter too. I warned them, but they just wouldn't listen. Neither of you have to die here today."

Guess we shouldn't have assumed they died of the virus. Seeing they'd been shot might have made us more cautious, at least. But if there's one thing I hate, it's a bully.

"I know you're not pointing that gun at my wife," says a

deep, familiar voice from behind Naomi. Dean steps out into the sunlight with a gun in each hand. One pointed at the creep and the other at the man standing by the car. "Let her go. Now."

Charlie walks out next, with his weapon moving between the two assholes. Like he can't quite decide who to shoot first.

Creep couldn't be any angrier. Two bright red spots stain his cheeks as his diabolical plan comes undone.

"You're outnumbered," says Dean in a calm voice. "Just in case you can't count."

"We're leaving," says the second man.

"What?" hisses Creep. "But Porter said—"

"Get in the car, Cody," says the guy with the shotgun.

Creep does as told, backing up toward their vehicle, keeping me as a shield between him and danger. When he gets close enough to the car, he dives in the passenger side, shoving me to the ground in the process. The muscle car tears out of the parking lot a moment later and it's over.

They're gone, thank goodness. And I was neither shot nor run over, which seems like a damn miracle.

Dean fires a few shots at the retreating vehicle, shattering the rear window. But I don't think he hit anyone. They don't slow down or stop, at any rate.

My heart is pounding inside my chest. But still. "Wife?"

"We can talk about it later," says Dean. "Are you hurt anywhere?"

"No."

His hands brush over me, checking just the same.

"I'm okay. Really."

His frown is the mightiest I've ever seen. "Let's get the last load and get out of here."

"They wanted to know where we were from."

"He kept asking," adds Naomi. "Was insistent about it. How many people we had and things like that. Of course we gave them nothing."

Dean pauses. "We need to make sure we're not followed."

CHAPTER TWELVE

WEDNESDAY

OUR ROUTE HOME TAKES US ON JUST ABOUT EVERY back road in the state. We stop regularly to check for any signs of a tail. I don't breathe easy until we're back with Sophie. There's no firepit tonight and all of the curtains are drawn to hide the light. The vibe is officially off.

Everyone over eighteen gathers in our living room while the girls hang out in Sophie's bedroom. They know we're being extra careful now due to outsiders. It's obvious, what with most everyone carrying a weapon. But there's no need to scare the crap out of them by letting them hear this conversation.

"He wanted to take us south," says Naomi.

"Dean heard about a group forming in that direction on the radio," I add. "It could be them."

He is, of course, standing over by the window so he can watch the street through a crack in the curtain again. The man loves to multitask. And he gives the forgotten bowl of food in my lap a meaningful look before speaking. "There's not much I can add. But that Cody guy was pissed when he couldn't take you two. He's not going to give up easy. We have to assume they're looking for us."

Dinner is rice and black beans with corn, sweet potato, lime, and green chilis. It's very good. I am just stressed out and distracted.

"None of us want to spend more time with dead bodies," says Naomi. "But I guess in the future, we need to be more careful and check if we can actually tell if they died from the flu or not."

Natalia sighs.

"Whoever shot them could have also been long gone." Leon shrugs. "This wasn't a failure on anyone's part."

"We should leave," says Avan. "Take the children and find somewhere safe away from these bastards."

"Like how we ran from the military base?" asks Reema. "What are the odds there are going to be people like this everywhere?"

"High," says Leon grimly.

Reema taps out a beat on the arm of her chair. "What we need is more people so we can defend this place properly."

Dean frowns, but he doesn't disagree. "In the meantime, I want to double up on the watch. I don't like the idea of anyone alone out there. One person watches the road into town and the other walks the length of Church Street and Oak Street. Both with the walkie-talkies and binoculars. You'll be in view of each other the whole time. But from the ends of those streets, you can pretty much see the other half of town. Hopefully if anyone is trying to sneak up on us, we'll see them."

THURSDAY

Watches are decided randomly. Dean and I are allotted the last one of the night. Which means we get a decent amount of sleep before being out there. So long as we're able to not lie awake staring at the ceiling, stressing about the situation, of course. I managed to get a few hours.

No idea when I last saw the dawn. The sky full of stars fading as the horizon changes color. From black and gray to purple and blue. Then orange and gold as the day begins again. Birds start singing and the world awakens. It's a beautiful thing.

I stand guard by the school bus. It keeps you mostly out of sight, but able to watch the road into town. Dean takes his turn doing the walk down Church and Oak. We both wear walkie-talkies and pistols strapped to our belts. My black leather jacket is done up all the way and a blue cotton scarf wrapped around my neck against the cool morning air.

Dean's steps are unhurried and steady. And his head turns this way and that, keeping a lookout for attack or any sign of danger. There's something about the set of his wide shoulders. It makes me feel like we're going to be okay. Or maybe it's my vagina talking. I don't know. He has somehow become my emotional support safety item. But I am definitely now focusing on the road into town. The threat against us is real and valid and I need to concentrate.

Sophie and Hazel are delighted to be having their much-asked-for sleepover. They're in one of the spare rooms at Natalia and Leon's. It made sense, since they got picked for the daytime watch. I went over and read them a chapter of the dragon book to help settle them down to sleep. However, the whispers and giggling probably went on until midnight. They were so excited.

I didn't used to have much to do with my neighbors. Nothing against them; life was just busy. People tended to come and go without me learning their names or much about them. I don't hate being part of a tight-knit community. It's nice to know we're all doing our best and looking out for each other. Losing most everyone you ever knew makes you appreciate people more.

The road leading into town is still empty—the same as it's been for the last hour. Mist rises from the ground as the sun slowly rises. Seems everything is silver and gold in the early hours. It's magical seeing the world wake up like this.

Dean strides toward me in his big-ass boots, blue jeans, and Henley. Such a serious face. No doubt he is worrying about how to protect everyone. Life was so much simpler when I hated him. My thirst for the man has always been apparent. But when lust turned to like turned to…I don't even know what this is. Shit sure got awkward fast.

"What?" he says.

"I was thinking about you."

"So you frowned."

"Yeah."

"Makes sense," he says. "Everything quiet?"

I just nod.

He is so pretty up close. The hard line of his jaw and the cut of his cheekbones. I love how rough his stubble feels under my fingertips. Heat radiates off his body and the temptation to lean into him is immense. To just bury my face in his chest for a minute and breathe deep. Comfort can be found there. I know it would make everything better.

And then there's the temptation to take a bite out of his thick neck. Never before have I been so weird about someone. Don't even get me started on my fascination with his mouth.

This is such a bad idea, me and him. The absolute worst. You would think the death of billions of people and the end of life as we know it would encourage me to make sounder decisions, but here we are. In all honesty, the possibility of my contributing to the gene pool *is* a real concern. Me and my nonsense need to be kept separate.

And I am staring so hard at him, it takes me a minute to notice him staring right back at me. He does nothing, however. Just stands there watching me, waiting to see what I'm going to do.

Nothing in this world should be taken for granted. We could die at any moment.

Fuck it.

With two handfuls of his shirt for purchase, I smash our mouths together.

There's nothing polite or nice about this. We're teeth and tongue. The taste of him goes straight to my head, and yes. I could happily do this for days. Strong hands cradle my head and hold me to him.

This has to be the best of all highs. He's made me an instant addict. I want to climb him and wrap myself up tight in his body. To crawl beneath his skin and make myself at home. Which is not like me at all. I don't just give myself away. You have to be careful. Take it slow so you don't get your heart broken. So some careless person doesn't shatter you into a thousand sharp pieces.

When I step back, we're both breathing hard. His hands curl into fists, like he has to stop himself from reaching for me.

Because we both want more. But there's no need to panic. We knew we had chemistry. This could still just be about sex. It's not like I'm in love with him, because that would be absolutely ridiculous.

He blows out a breath. "You have the absolute worst timing."

"Yeah."

"Do me a favor. Do that again later when I can do something about it, okay?"

"Um. I am going to go do the walk."

"Good idea," he says, turning to check out the road into town. But then he grabs me by the upper arm and drags me back behind the bus in a hurry. "Get down. Keep your head down."

But it's too little, too late. Because out of the bushes heading down to the creek on our right comes one of the men from yesterday. The one with long dark hair and tattoos. And he's pointing a semiautomatic in our direction as he walks out from between a couple of the cars we parked off road from the blockade.

Shit, shit, shit.

"You're outnumbered," shouts Cody the Creep. *He's* walking down the road toward us with three friends. "In case you can't count."

Dean swears beneath his breath.

The long-haired dude ushers us out of hiding. His face is as blank as can be. "Weapons on the ground. Slowly."

We both do as told. Dean turns as he kneels to place his weapon on the ground. Just enough for me to see the bulge down low in the back of his tee. He still has a gun tucked into the back waistband of his jeans.

The man keeps a careful eye on him, just waiting for him

to try something. And Dean's jaw is set and his shoulders are heaving. Like the minute he sees an opening, he is going to tear them to pieces.

"I don't blame you for being distracted. But no one's going to hurt her," says the stranger in a low voice. "Just stay calm and we get out of this in one piece."

"Are you sure about that?" mutters Dean.

"So good to see you again," says Cody as he gets within chatting distance. Such a fucking creep. "Where's your other friend? The redhead with the nice tits? Not that it matters. Nash here told me there's ten or so in your group, and I cannot wait to meet them all. See who might be of interest to us and who belongs in a hole in the ground. Not going to lie to you, big guy. That's probably where you're headed. Because Porter sure did like what he heard about your wife. He can't *wait* to meet her."

Two of the new men with him look me over with prurient interest. One even licks his lips. *Ew.* But the third stares glassy-eyed off into the distance. No idea what he's on, but he's feeling the effects big time.

I refuse to be afraid of these dicks. No matter how much my hands are shaking. And my big mouth gave us an opportunity to escape last time. I wonder if it might work its magic again. "Oh, so you guys are like his errand boys? That must make you feel really important."

Dean sighs and says, "Baby..."

Cody sneers and raises his hand.

But the one with the gun on us, Nash, says, "Porter wanted her unmarked and in one piece."

"Fuck's sake. Where's the kid?" Cody asks Nash.

"Told him to wait back in the bushes."

"Thought the whole fucking reason you wanted him along was so he could learn how we worked."

"He doesn't need to see this," says Nash—smoothly moving his aim to Cody.

It all happens so quickly. None of the four men he came with even manage to raise their weapons in time. Nash takes out three of his companions with a single shot to each. The fourth is dropped by Dean with his hidden handgun. Blood blossoms between their eyes and all of the men fall limply to the asphalt.

Whoa.

Birds startled by the sound of the guns take flight from nearby trees. The sounds of shouting and doors slamming come from the small town waking up in a hurry behind us.

But calm as can be, Nash sets down his weapon, along with a variety of other guns and knives. Like, a whole lot of them. He's done what he set out to do, apparently.

Dean wastes no time scooping up his other pistol and putting me behind him. "What the fuck is happening here?"

Hands held up high, Nash stands still. "I'm going to call to the boy. Then you'll understand. But don't hurt him—he's not armed, he's just a child."

Dean nods. "Do it."

"Bowie," calls Nash. "Come on out now. Take it nice and slow."

And from out of some bushes back down the road appears said child. He's ten or so. Around the same age as Hazel. His skin is white and his hair dark, and his eyes are as wide as can be.

"Bowie?" I ask with a smile. "That's your name?"

He nods like his head has come loose. His gaze goes to the bodies on the ground, and his face turns even whiter, if possible. "You killed Cody."

"Cody was an asshole," says Nash.

"Yeah," says the boy in little more than a whisper. "But Porter's going to be pissed."

"We're not going back to Porter, buddy."

"We're not?" he asks, and he sounds hopeful.

Charlie reaches us first, wearing pajama pants, in bare feet, carrying a pistol. His hair is sticking out in every direction. Just truly impressive bed hair. But the last thing we need is someone getting spooked and starting shooting. There's been enough death already this morning.

"It's okay," I say. "We're okay."

Dean's dark brows are drawn tight together. He is seriously unhappy. And he's still pointing his gun at Nash when he says, "Talk fast."

"Can we expect more visitors?" asks Leon.

We're gathered in the dining room of the bed-and-breakfast. It made sense to be inside, out of view. The three children are having breakfast with Charlie and Avan in the kitchen. But the rest of us are gathered to hear what this stranger has to say. He's seated in the corner with all eyes on him. Dean checked to make sure he wasn't hiding any other weapons. However, tensions are still sky high.

"No," says Nash. "I followed you from the home store yesterday. It wasn't easy. Lost you a time or two, but by then I had the general direction figured out. Cody didn't even tell Porter exactly where you were. The drugs he was taking made him paranoid as fuck. And he wanted all of the glory for bringing women back to the camp."

"You were with those people," says Reema. "Why should we trust anything you say?"

Nash's mouth is set in a serious line. "Let me explain. I saw them last week when I was grabbing a few things in Sonoma. This pack of assholes emptying a grocery store. It would have been easy enough to avoid them. But then I saw Bowie and got a bad feeling. One of them started pushing him around and slapping him and…there were too many of them for me to safely get him out of there. But I couldn't just leave him with them."

"That speaks well of you," says Natalia.

"Thank you, ma'am," says Nash, subdued for some reason. Guess he doesn't take praise well. "I followed them back to their camp. There were about thirty of them, and—"

"Thirty?" I ask in surprise.

"Yeah. Porter got active on the radio and putting up signs early on, asking people to join him. Most were just happy to find other survivors and some sort of organization after all the chaos. But from what I heard, about half made a run for it when they realized what he was *really* like. How things were going to be. Anyone with a woman to protect got them the hell out of there. He'd tightened up security with people loyal to him by the time I joined. Slipping out or moving around at night was more difficult."

"Where is he based?" asks Dean.

"He took over a winery outside of Sonoma. Stocked up on weapons, food, and pharmaceuticals."

"If he's down in Sonoma, why in the hell does he care about a hardware depot an hour north?" Leon shakes his head. "No wonder he doesn't have permanent security on these places he's claimed if they're so spread out."

"Anything people are going to need to survive, he wants," says Nash. "Plus, they work as bait. His men also check the hardware warehouse to the south of them, and any grocery stores between the two that they haven't yet managed to remove all of the stock from. Guess he thinks they're bound to come across some people they can bring back to camp."

Natalia clicks her tongue. "Greed and power. The world ends and still everything stays the same."

Leon gives her hand a comforting squeeze.

"You must have felt strongly about the child to have joined them," says Reema.

"I remember what it's like being that size, ma'am. Too small to fight back." Nash clears his throat. "I was a bounty hunter for a while. Porter wanted my skills, but I was new, so he didn't trust me. First opportunity I had to get Bowie out safely was when Cody told Porter we had a lead on this place. I talked Cody into thinking this would be a good chance to show the kid how things are done."

Dean stares at the man in thought for a minute. "You want to stay here with Bowie?"

Leon narrows his gaze on the stranger.

"Just long enough to make sure he's protected," says Nash. "He needs a family. But Porter knows we ran into you outside Santa Rosa. He knows you're out here somewhere, and he has nothing better to do than keep looking."

"He's going to have to be dealt with," says Dean.

I just nod. Because from everything we've seen and heard, the likelihood of him letting us live in peace is as low as can be.

"We need more people to keep this place safe," says Natalia.

"You do," agrees Nash. "And I have some ideas about where you can find them."

CHAPTER THIRTEEN

"**E**LEVEN OUT OF TEN," I ANNOUNCE WITH THE UTMOST authority.

Hazel and Sophie fall about laughing. Even Bowie manages a small smile. We're hanging out in the backyard of our house having a handstand competition. It's been a strange day, starting off with a bang. I long for the times when death and dead bodies weren't the normal. But here we are. Sunset isn't for another couple of hours yet. We decided to get together and eat early. Have everyone inside their houses with the curtains drawn, blocking out any light, before dusk. Just to be safe.

The watch is continuing, of course. We're now each doing duty twice every twenty-four hours. Once during the day and once at night. If the figures Nash gave us are right, then there's no way we can stop Porter and all of his people, should they find us. But we can give each other warning and hopefully get the children safely out of town.

Hazel sets her hands on her hips. "That handstand was a *twelve* out of ten."

"I'll give you thirteen out of ten and that is my absolute last offer," I say, waving a wooden spoon at the girls. Which sets off the giggling all over again. They are so high on life and it's beautiful to see.

"You cannot be serious." Avan shakes his head with much woe. "That handstand was clearly a fourteen. I've never seen such a spectacularly upside-down person!"

"Oh no," I say. "There's a dispute between the judges. What are we going to do?"

"More handstands," shouts Sophie with glee.

I wish my phone hadn't died. It would be good to have some pictures of times like this. The girls smiling in the late afternoon light.

We spent most of the day working in the garden. Dean didn't want Nash helping with the bodies, in case he took the opportunity to pick up a knife or something in one of the houses. Given what happened this morning, and what he told us, it seems unlikely. And if he wanted to cause trouble, he could do it with his hands. But trust takes time. Leon helped with the gardening today too. Though he was mostly there to keep an eye on Nash.

Reema spent an hour or so teaching the children about photosynthesis and pollination and other garden-relevant science. They loved the attention, and they loved listening to her. She must have been amazing at her job because she's an exceptional speaker. And she seemed to enjoy it too.

Bowie and the girls also dug in the dirt, searching for worms for a while. It was part of learning about composting and soil quality. He seemed okay so long as Nash was near. Which is fair enough, given he's the one constant in the child's life right now. Currently, they're seated together on the edge of the back porch, watching the handstand competition.

Nash wants to use the radio to contact some friends who might be interested in joining our small town. People who know how to help us keep everyone safe. It sounds good in theory. But we've known him for approximately five minutes. And in that time he's pointed a gun at us twice. Life continues to be complicated in new and strange ways. But a population of twelve, with three of those people being children, can't survive against thirty assholes.

Drastic measures must be taken.

In the meantime, dinner is canned ham and pineapple fried rice cooked on a camp stove. Avan and I are in charge. Natalia, Reema, and Naomi are gathered on the cane porch chairs, keeping an eye on Nash while discussing recent events. Charlie and Leon are on watch.

And Dean is walking back from his afternoon wash at the creek. His dark wet hair slicked back with those hints of silver showing. Blue jeans riding low on his hips and his bare chest…huh. He sure is a healthy specimen. There are pecs and nipples and abs and all of that. And I am not drooling. My saliva production just got away from me for a minute.

One scar curls around his side. But I think the bulk of them are on his back. His shoulders and biceps flex as he pulls a tee on over his head. The view of his bare chest is going, going, gone. So sad. Woe is me. How dare he make *me* wet too. And the kicker is the way his steady gaze stays on me the entire time. He knows exactly what he's doing. Manipulating my hormones in this way is the work of a cad.

"Fuck me," mutters Naomi. She's such a harlot after my own heart.

Though it's not like Natalia and Reema and Avan aren't staring too. The only adult who seems unimpressed by the display is Nash. I believe he mumbles something involving the words "show" and "pony." But I can't quite catch what he says.

"Dean, watch this!" shouts Sophie as the girls perform a series of cartwheels and handstands.

"Excellent work," he says. "I swear you guys are getting better at this stuff every day. You must be the best gymnasts in the whole wide world."

Hazel and Sophie soak up the praise.

Then he walks straight up to me and says, "Mind if we talk for a minute inside?"

"Sure."

He takes my hand and leads me through the back door and into the kitchen, where we then take a turn into the hallway. Here, he stops and stares down at me. "I need you to do something for me."

"What?"

"You know how much I love your mouth and your mind. But you've got to stop saying shit to bad guys that makes them want to hit you," he says in a calm voice. "Please. I can feel it giving me new gray hairs every time you do it."

My shoulders drop. "I don't mean to."

"But you kind of do."

"They're just such assholes."

He nods. "I know they are. Doesn't stop sarcasm from being a bad defense against a fist."

I rest my back against the wall and sigh. "Fine."

"Thank you. I appreciate it." He's still holding the hand he led me inside by. But he's not touching me otherwise. Just standing there watching me with those dark blue eyes of his. There's an intimacy to this—me and him standing alone in the shadows having a stolen moment. "How was your day?"

"The horrors persist, but so do I."

"Good job."

"We did gardening," I say. "I made Nash haul buckets of water. That was fun for me."

The frown descends. "I don't like him being around you."

"He was fine. Bowie wanted to hang out with the girls and Nash is his security blanket, so..." I take a deep breath. "You called me 'baby' this morning."

"Yeah."

"And you called me 'wife' yesterday."

He nods. "Yes, I did."

"And 'love' came out of your mouth before. You need to stop making it weird between us."

"Honestly it seems a little late for that, given everything." He winces and thinks it over. "Can't help but notice you don't seem actually upset by me using any of this language."

"Not *upset* exactly. *Perturbed* might be a better word."

"Hmm."

I don't know what to say or do with all of this. Which is a lie. So many years of trying to make emotionally backward boys feel something besides lust for me. To stop playing games and cheating and ghosting me. This man is not without his issues. Truly. But he's devoted to me in a way I've never experienced before.

"Are you even the smallest bit interested in Naomi?" I ask out of curiosity. "I mean, she's so cool."

"Interested in what way?"

"You know."

He cocks his head and stares down at me in wide-eyed wonder. Then he lifts his hand and strokes my neck. His gentle touch soon turns firm, however, as he holds my neck in his grasp. I don't know if I should be okay with this. But the side of his thumb slides over my skin and I don't hate it. Not even a little.

"What?" I ask.

His hand returns to his side. "Don't get me wrong, I kind of like that you're jealous. But where the hell do you think I'm getting the time and energy from to chase after anyone's ass but yours?"

After a pause, I admit, "Actually, that's valid."

He grunts.

"You had to kill someone again," I say. "Are you okay with that?"

"They came here looking to cause harm. It won't cost me any sleep. Does that bother you?"

"No. I don't think so. You did what you had to."

"And I'd do it again. No one hurts you or Sophie. I won't allow it."

Time for a change of topic. "What do you miss from the old world today?"

"That's easy." His smile is there and gone. "Hot showers."

I happy sigh at the memory of same. "I could do with a really good facial. Want to have a spa night with me sometime?"

"Sure."

"You any good at painting nails?"

"Doubt it," he says. "But I am willing to try. What are you grateful for?"

"We're still all together and in one piece. That seems sort of huge given everything."

"Yeah."

I step into him and slide my hands beneath his tee. My hands wind around his waist and across his back. And I hold on good and tight just because I can. Today involved having the shit scared out of me. I deserve a moment or more of goodness with him.

"We're hugging?" he asks with interest.

"Yes."

And his arms come around me. He doesn't even attempt to grope my ass or anything. Just respects what we're doing. Never underestimate the curative effects of a forehead kiss. "This is nice. I like this."

"Me too."

One of my hands drifts over the tangle of scars on his back. I don't like that he was hurt. His skin is cool to the touch. He's still warming up after the cold water from the creek. And he smells of the soap and whatever he washed his hair with. This is a top-tier experience, being this close to him, hearing his heart beat strong and sure inside his chest. Would do it again.

Mind you, we're doing this in the wrong order. Hugging should probably come before kissing. But nothing could make this more special.

Something that is proven wrong when Sophie plows into

us, joining in the hug. The girl could have had a serious career ahead of her as a linebacker. She wriggles in between us with a smile.

Nash and Bowie are set up across the street from us. It's a new wooden two-bedroom house with big windows to let in the light. Of course, the curtains are drawn for now. We haven't even dared use the generator we picked up at the hardware warehouse, due to fear of the noise it would make. Having the power to run a fridge or heat some water for a hot shower would be amazing. But it's just not worth the risk.

We gather in the living room of their new home. Reema, Leon, Dean, and I. Natalia is watching the girls again. She's fast become a favorite. Charlie is catching up on sleep while Avan and Naomi are on watch. Things are changing so fast. Starting out the day as enemies with Nash and now working together to provide a safe home for everyone makes for a steep learning curve. Dean's protective instincts have gone into overdrive. And I know this because he's hovering, standing behind me, glowering if Nash so much as looks my way. Which is highly unnecessary.

But big feelings continue to be a challenge for both of us, it seems. Emotional growth during the apocalypse is a thorny thing.

Nash has the radio on his lap and is holding the microphone. He and his friends agreed to talk at a certain time of night. They're apparently preppers who had been planning for the end of the world. People who cut off physical contact with the outside when news of the virus started to spread.

"George?" he asks into the microphone. "Pedro?"

"Was wondering when you'd turn up again," says someone back. "You owe me twenty, old man."

Nash's laughter is low and rough. "You bet against me, George?"

"It'd been almost a week. How was I to know you weren't lying dead in a ditch?" asks someone in a crotchety tone.

"What happened?" asks the first person. Pedro. "Run into trouble?"

"You could say that," answers Nash. "Question is…how bored are you two of sitting in your bunkers and basements?"

"Bored?" asks Pedro. "Wash your mouth out with soap. I've barely started rereading my twenty years of back issues of *Gunsmith Monthly*. And Trish has only threatened to divorce George eight times over his choice of contentious words in Scrabble."

"It's up to nine after this morning, and I mean it this time," says a female voice. "I don't care if *za* is allowed or not. We don't use it in our games!"

George gives a long-suffering sigh. "Okay, yes. We are bored as hell. We spent twenty years prepping for the end of the world. We prepared so well that now that it's arrived, we have nothing that needs doing. What have you got on offer, Nash?"

"Oh, nothing," he responds. "Just a good old-fashioned war."

FRIDAY

The meeting was held the next day in a town on the coast. Somewhere that was unlikely to be of interest to Porter. Dean, Reema, Leon, and Nash were in attendance. It obviously went well, since the convoy returned under the cover of darkness. They made the drive here by the light of the full moon with no headlights on. Dean and Nash's vehicle was up first, so no one would freak out and think we're under attack. Not that it's easy to see which vehicle is which. We communicated by radio throughout the day. They let us know to move the cars blocking the road. These are the times we live in.

And this situation with the town has got to be causing Dean actual physical pain. Letting so many new people in so quickly. But the worry of possible attack from within doesn't beat the ticking time bomb that is Porter.

"What are preppers like?" Sophie stands beside me, holding my hand. She's dressed in plaid pajamas and tennis shoes with a cardigan against the cool night air.

"I think they're people who like to be organized. Who want to know that they have plans and supplies in case things go wrong. And doing that is a big part of their life."

She thinks this over for a moment. "Things went really wrong."

"Yeah," I say. "They sure did."

"Do you think they might have some of that freeze-dried ice cream?" she asks. "Bowie wants to try some."

Bowie sits on the grass nearby, listening to our conversation and tossing a tennis ball into the air. He wasn't happy about not going to the meeting today. But Nash thought he was safer here. I hate how Bowie is sort of scared of us. Whatever treatment he endured at Porter's camp makes my blood boil. He's just a child. You'd have to be an asshole to hurt him. Just another good excuse to shoot Porter, in my opinion. Not something I thought I would ever be thinking. I cannot find it in me to regret it, however. The apocalypse makes certain issues very plain and simple.

"It sounds good," says Bowie. Which is a miracle, given it's the most he's said to me all day.

"I don't know if they'll have any." I give him a smile. "We can certainly ask, though. If anyone has some, it'll be preppers."

Avan gave the children a lesson in the importance of hygiene and basic wound treatment to stop infection. Then they tried out some of the craft sets from the hardware warehouse before helping us sort canned foods for a while. Everyone's home has enough provisions for now, so we decided to convert one of the houses into our general storage space. It makes for a less obvious target in case people like Porter arrive, who are out to steal us and/or our supplies. And it keeps everything closer to us since the grocery store is out on the edge of town.

But now everyone is waiting to meet the new people. Most of them are gathered in Natalia and Leon's house, out of the wind. Only Naomi and the two children and me are outside. Hazel gave up and went inside a while back.

We don't risk any flashlights. My vision has adjusted well enough to the darkness, however. There are two SUVs and an RV, along with our two pickup trucks. The sounds of car doors opening and closing and muted conversation fills the night air. From out of the front of the RV comes an older white couple with gray hair. Wearing a dress and a rifle is a bold choice, but it works. The man is wiry, with his hair tied back in a ponytail. His gaze roves the town, taking note of everything. My guess is they're Trisha and George.

"Dean!" shouts Sophie, and she's off and running.

No one needs to know the immense relief I feel, having him

back within reach. It can stay a secret between me and my foolish heart. Sophie collides with him at full speed. The smiles seem to come easier for him these days. Which is nice. He gives me a chin tip, and I nod in return. Everything is fine now.

Bowie is also on his feet and heading over to Nash. The tension seems to fall straight out of him at the sight of the man. One day he's going to feel the same confidence and security all of the time.

Trisha wanders over to me, her gaze following the same path as mine. "Don't you worry," she says. "We're going to help you keep these babies safe and sound."

CHAPTER FOURTEEN

FRIDAY

"**W**E THOUGHT WE WERE JUST GETTING A WEEK OR two off school," says Wyatt. "Then everyone actually goes and dies."

Trisha and George have two grandsons. Eighteen-year-old twins, Wyatt and Jack. Both of them tall with long blond hair. Their parents died in a car accident a couple of years ago.

"Who could have guessed Grandma and Grandpa had a clue?" asks Jack.

Trisha gives them a patient smile. "I know it hurts your souls to admit that, boys."

"Just really looking forward to the teenage years," mutters Dean.

Natalia and Leon's house is crowded with people. Charlie and Avan volunteered to keep watch, but everyone else is present. The children are in the spare bedroom watching a movie on a working laptop provided by Jack. They couldn't be more excited to get back in touch with technology, even if there's no internet. You would think they'd been living in the Dark Ages..

Pedro is a handsome fifty-year-old veteran with brown skin. He's accompanied by a German shepherd named Honey. Ignore the humans. She is hands down the most important addition to the town, according to the children. "So tomorrow we get the rest of the dead in the ground, get some security cameras up around town, and figure out how to deal with this asshole and his people," says Pedro. "Sound like a plan?"

Natalia sips at a cup of coffee. "It's as good a place to start as any. The houses on this street have been cleared. But some of them might need more of an airing. You'll want to judge that for yourself."

"You got a place with a hot tub for us, right?" asks Wyatt.

Jack nods. "It's a need, not a want."

"There actually is one," I say in bemusement.

"Please don't encourage them," pleads Trisha with a pained expression.

"Pretty lady, give us all the details." No idea which of the twins said it. But they're both giving me the most flirtatious grins.

Standing beside me, Dean crosses his arms over his chest. He doesn't seem quite so amused for some reason.

George squeezes his eyelids shut tight like he has a headache. I know they mentioned threats of divorce over Scrabble issues as a reason to leave their bunker. But I would pay good money to know how many times the lives of the twins had been threatened by their grandparents due to the boys' big mouths and excitable attitudes.

"You two are on watch for the rest of the night," says George. "Go on."

This sets off a lot of moaning and groaning from the pair. Like *a lot*.

"I'll relieve you at two," says Pedro.

"Thank fuck for that," mumbles Jack, as he and his brother head for the door. "We owe you, man."

Pedro smothers a smile. "Yeah, yeah."

"We usually share the watch around in two- to three-hour lots," says Dean.

But Pedro shakes his head. "Don't bother. I don't sleep for shit anyway. If I manage a couple of hours it's a good night."

"Why don't I keep you company," offers Naomi.

Pedro gives her a nod. "I'd like that."

And so Wolf Creek's population goes up to seventeen.

Dean stands in the doorway to my bedroom. Navy pajama pants sit low on his hips and an old white tee covers his chest. He's frowning for some reason. "I've never been in your bedroom before."

"Haven't you?"

"No," he says. "Am I allowed to be here?"

"Yes."

It's eleven o'clock or so. Sophie is fast asleep and the world is quiet. We stayed for a while at Natalia and Leon's, talking to the new people. And giving the children time to finish their film.

You would think I had bear traps laid out on the floor with the careful way he wanders inside. The room has a solid wooden four-poster bed with white linens. There's devil's ivy growing in a wine bottle filled with water. Which is how it survived the apocalypse and lack of care for a while. And a couple of framed black-and-white photos of trees on the wall taken from interesting angles. Along with a cool old glass chandelier-type light fixture it would be nice to see working someday.

But of course, I'm using a couple of pillar candles sitting on a plate on the bedside table to see what I'm doing. Which is lying on the bed in a pair of plaid boxer shorts and a tank top, reading a book on companion planting. I am determined to develop a green thumb. Like my life depends on it. Because once all of the canned food runs out, it will.

"Do you like all of this?" he asks, indicating the furniture and décor.

I nod.

"Good."

"Things feel a little less stressy tonight," I say. "Five new people who I'm guessing know how to help with our situation."

"They know how," he confirms. "George wouldn't allow us to see the location of his setup. We had to wait outside of town while they packed up their stuff. But Pedro showed us the basement where he'd been sheltering in place. Could have comfortably lived there for a decade and defended it for at least as long. He had a lot of weapons. Not a tank, though."

"Remember, it's good to share your toys with your friends."

He gives me a look. "No. It's my tank. They can get their own."

I just smile.

"I don't know why I didn't think of it earlier," says Dean. "We need a dog like Honey."

"That's a great idea. Soph would love one."

"No. I mean for security. The house you've chosen—"

"The house *we've* chosen."

"Whatever. It isn't very defensible. There's no perimeter. We're not hidden during the day, and even at night there's light and noise that betray where we are. We're too exposed."

"And a dog would help defend us?" I ask. "Are they really that dangerous if people have guns?"

"As a fast-moving threat, yes. But literally any dog that can bark is a help," he says. "They hear everything. They can smell strangers, even after they've slipped away. Some dogs can even track if they catch a scent. Dogs make us a hard target."

I think it over. "There must have been some dogs in town originally. They either died from lack of water if they were locked inside or wandered away if their food ran out. But they might not have wandered too far."

"We should start looking. Leave some food out on the edges of town and see if any show up."

"That's a good idea. Come here," I say, patting the empty mattress beside me.

He pauses, and his mouth opens and closes. Like he's not sure what to say. Then he wisely shuts his mouth and lies down beside me. I don't think I have ever seen him look so ill at ease. The man absolutely believes I am setting him up for annihilation. That he will say or do the wrong thing and be banished from my sight.

"Look." I point to the white-painted ceiling high above our heads. "Do you see?"

It takes him a moment, but then he understands. "Somebody drew stars up there with a pencil."

"Yeah, and a crescent moon."

"Huh." And a small smile curves his mouth. From this

distance the bruises beneath his eyes are obvious. He's had another long day in a series of them lately.

"Close your eyes. Go to sleep. You look tired."

He snorts. "Astrid."

"What?"

"I am not getting any sleep lying on a bed with you the way things are between us." He sits up and swings his legs over the side of the bed.

My limb isn't *exactly* working of its own volition. However, I don't remember making the decision to grab hold of the back of his shirt to stop him.

He gives me this look over his shoulder like he doesn't know what's going on, and honestly, me too. The words that come out of my mouth, though, make perfect sense.

"I don't want you to leave."

He pauses, and his expression is so controlled. I hate how he's holding back and hiding whatever he's feeling. How fucking dare he do that when I clearly can't. "What do you want, then?" he asks.

"I already told you. I don't want you to leave."

"And what does that involve for you? What does it look like…me staying in this bed with you?"

"Oh, fuck you," I say with wonder, pushing myself up into a sitting position. "You want to do a lecture series on consent now?"

He shrugs. "Better late than never."

"Go fuck yourself."

"Apparently I don't have to," he says, with no small amount of delight, because he is such an asshole. And he's all mine.

With a hand wrapped around his thick neck for leverage,

I am now where I want to be. Where I want *him* to be. Which is with me straddling his lap and our mouths smashed together. Because there's nothing nice or gentle about this. It was highly unlikely there ever would be. From day one, we've been messed up in a variety of ways. In a normal world, he'd be in jail and I'd be in therapy. But here we are. He's made me furious and feverish and a thousand other things besides.

His hands are in my hair and his tongue is in my mouth. I can never get close enough to him. The need to feel his stubble scraping my skin. To taste toothpaste and him…whatever the hell that is. I don't know, but I need it now. And he's obviously thinking the same thing, since my tank top is gone and soon his tee is too.

Shit. "Dean," I say. "The door."

"Right. Legs around me." With a hand beneath my ass, he stands and takes the necessary few steps to close the bedroom door. "Done."

"We have to remember to be quiet."

He raises a brow at me. "You think you can be quiet?"

"That wasn't a challenge."

"Sort of sounded like one," he says, throwing me on the bed. My back bounces against the mattress. He has my boxer shorts off me and is climbing between my spread legs with a feral smile I do not trust in the least. Not one iota. "Here, use this cushion."

And I take the offered pillow because I'm not a fool. This man has a tendency to keep his word. Having him gaze at me this way has got me hot and flustered. Being laid out naked before him for the first time like this is something. I don't want to be nervous or anything. Now is the time to be bold and beautiful and words like that. However, it takes me a moment to find my confidence and stare back at him with all of the want and need inside of me.

"You really are the prettiest fucking thing I've ever seen. I could just stare at you for the rest of my days." His hand loosely grips my throat before trailing down between my breasts. Each inch of me lights up. Nerve endings coming to life at his touch. "We do this, then I am in here from now on, Astrid. When we have problems, we work them out together."

"Okay."

His fingertips trace a path over my belly and down to my mound. Then he shuffles back, making room for himself on the end of the bed. Hands slide beneath my ass cheeks and he gives my sex reverent, sweet, closed-mouth kisses. Nice-to-meet-you, getting-to-know-you sort of kisses. Already my skin feels a size too small. Like all the things he inspires inside of me can't possibly be contained.

His thumbs hold back the lips of my sex, and he really gets to work.

I feel everything he's doing to me as if it's magnified. Enhanced in some way. It's not just that he knows what he's doing. And he very much does. From the long, sweeping laps with the flat of his tongue to the sucking pulls of his lips on my clitoris.

Sensation builds at the base of my spine, and I bow my back trying to keep some sort of control. His fingers have a bruisingly tight grip of my ass cheeks. There's no escaping the intensity of what he's doing. How he fucks me with his tongue and teases around the ever-tightening bud of my clit. There'll be stubble rash on my inner thighs tomorrow and I absolutely do not care.

I remember the cushion just in time. My whole body tenses and crashes from some impossible height as it hits me. I am nothing and nowhere and everything at once. The way my body and brain are in tiny pieces floating up amongst the stars. Surviving the end of the world just for that single orgasm is honestly valid.

Which is what I'm thinking when the pillow is removed from my face. He is standing beside the bed. I choose not to begrudge him the small, satisfied smile. Just this once. He wipes his mouth with his discarded tee and asks, "More? Or are you done?"

It takes a moment to bring my brain back online. "The first one. Lose the pants."

"Whatever you want."

He eases them over his hard-on before letting them fall to the floor. And I honestly love how getting me off got him so excited. Dean in all his glory is a thing of beauty. But then, he always is, dressed *or* naked. And he allows me to ogle him by candlelight. The sharp lines of his face and the lean power of his muscular body. And the scars that tell such a story of survival and pain. I don't think there's ever been anything more spectacular than him standing there with his hair all messed up because of my hands.

His dick is slightly thicker and longer than average. Given the way he watches me as he climbs back onto the bed, I have no doubt he knows how to use it.

There's the strangest sensation of coming home. With my arms around his neck and legs around his body, he lines the wide, blunt head of his cock up with my opening and pushes in slow and steady. We both catch our breath.

With his hips against mine, he rests his face in my neck and groans. Such a sweet and deep sound. It's like I feel it resonating in my soul. There's no room for worries or doubts when he's with me. My fingers thread through his hair, holding him as close as can be.

"Shit," he mutters, and lifts his head. "Condom. No wonder you feel so fucking good."

It takes a minute for the feel-good hormones to calm down so I can think straight. "Oh. Um. Contraceptive injection is good for another five weeks yet. I was clear the last time I tested. No unsafe sex ever. How about you?"

"Same and same."

"We seem to have a certain effect on each other…"

"I've noticed," he says. "Are you sure?"

I nod, and his sudden grin is sort of manic. His mouth finds mine, and we're kissing deep and messy. My tongue tangling with his and our teeth clashing. One of us starts biting, but I am not naming names. He takes his weight on one arm and grabs my thigh with the hand from the other.

This is no lovemaking. We're fucking and claiming and owning each other. And the feel of him surging deep is ecstatic. Sweat beads on both of our skins as our bodies crash together. There's no need to be gentle right now. Not when his growls and groans are wrecking me. The fierce emotion in his eyes is inescapable. You dream of someone who wants you this way. Like you're their world and their wish all rolled up into one. But to actually find them seems so impossible.

His thick cock is lighting me up from top to toe. Dragging

over so many nerve endings and delicate muscles inside of me. All of which have been neglected for far too long. Then the solid heat of him hits something deep within me, and oh! My mouth falls open and electricity sings in my veins.

He bares his teeth at me like an animal and does it again and again. The man fucks me into the mattress like this is his job now. And I am here to say this is definitely his job now.

In lieu of the cushion, I bite his shoulder as I come. Happily, he seems to like being bitten because his hips buck hard against me one, two, three times as he comes too. So nice when kinks align.

The scents of sweat and sex fill the room. He draws his semihard cock out of me and collapses onto the mattress at my side. How is his dick not exhausted? Seriously. It's ridiculous.

The only sound is us both panting. My muscles are so relaxed any movement seems extreme, but the night air is making its presence known against my cooling skin. So I reach for the blanket and pull it over us.

It seems a shame to waste a warm, naked man. Also, not to be clingy, but I feel like being clingy. I throw a leg over his middle and an arm over his chest and just generally get comfortable. And that's definitely me done for the night. If he wants to go again he can wait for the morning. Because it was a long-ass day.

Dean wraps an arm around my shoulders. "Okay," he says.

"Okay what?"

"No. It was a question. Are you okay?" he asks.

"Yes. Are you?"

"Yeah."

I sit up long enough to blow out the candles, then

return to my previous position. He's surprisingly comforta-ble. Usually, I am a solo sleeper and don't like or need a lot of post-sex touching. But I am liking this so far, cuddling up to him in the dark.

"You know I love you, right?" he asks out of nowhere.

"What? No, you don't. And you can't just say that."

"Too late. I do and I already did." The asshole is abso-lutely smiling. I can hear it in his voice. "But just out of inter-est, why can't I?"

"Well…it's too soon, for starters."

"Some people know at first sight," he says. "What else have you got?"

"Saying it the first time we have sex is really dubious. You lack all credibility."

"Wouldn't that be if I told you I loved you *before* we had sex? I said it after, so my intentions are pure and I'm in the clear," he says. When I don't respond, he asks, "What are you thinking?"

"That if I kill you now I wouldn't have to go to jail."

"But you'd miss me, and Sophie would be really sad."

I sigh.

"That escalated quickly. Why is this such an issue for you?" he asks. "Is this about the kidnapping thing?"

"The kidnapping thing."

"Is it?"

I take a deep breath and let it out slowly. "No. Honestly, so much has happened. I kind of feel like we're past all that."

"Good. That's good. Then what is it?"

"No one has romantically said they love me before, and this…it doesn't feel right for some reason."

"I'm sorry it doesn't feel right," he says. "But I can absolutely assure you that it's real. I know that because *I've* never said it romantically to someone before. You're the first."

"You've never said it before?"

"No. Never."

I hold on to him a tighter in the quiet darkness for some reason. Let's not examine why. "Okay."

# CHAPTER FIFTEEN

SATURDAY

WITH THE EXTRA HELP FOR WATCHES, DEAN IS ABLE to get to work on the solar power situation with no distractions. And Trisha is skilled at electricals and lends a hand. Only a couple of houses in town have solar panels installed. They're able to get the ones on our designated storage building back up and working. It makes for a perfect space to monitor our new security cameras. Hopefully they'll also allow us to run a fridge in future. Making sure the town security upgrade works comes first, though. Then they change out the fried battery at our place. Our solar panels will be used to power walkie-talkies and such for now.

I spend the day helping with the last great push to deal with our dead. And the job is as sad and awful as you'd imagine. By the end of the day, every muscle in me hurts and I am never getting the scent of rotting bodies out of my head. But with the extra hands, we're able to commit the rest of our dead to the ground. This feels like a strange thing to celebrate. However, at the end of the world, you have to take your wins where you can. And this includes the living now outnumbering the dead above ground in Wolf Creek.

Natalia does some bird-watching and math with the children in the morning. Honey the German shepherd escorts them around town. Then they run around chasing each other for a while before watching more movies in the afternoon. Somewhere between these two activities, Bowie finds a skateboard and promptly falls off same. Meaning Avan has his first patient and Bowie gets a cut on his elbow glued back together.

We gather in the bed-and-breakfast at night. Their living room is still big enough for all of us and the fireplace is epic. The curtains are drawn since we're still being security conscious. Canned chicken and vegetables with ramen is for dinner. Wyatt and Jack seem enamored of our bountiful supply of liquor. Same goes for the lack of a legal drinking age. But after a shot of bourbon, Trisha gives them a look and there's no more of that. They're good boys at heart, even if their egos and mouths are as wide as the nearest ocean.

George and Leon are manning the security/supplies command center. They wanted to check out which angles were and weren't covered by the cameras. What changes might be needed. There was talk of taking turns, with one of them at the monitors while the other went outside and stood in various positions. Then they'd discuss it all via walkie-talkie. It's the kind of testing our system needs, no doubt.

We're seated on a sofa watching the children slowly run out of steam. Hazel and Sophie are busy teaching Bowie how to make friendship bracelets in a corner of the room. The boy sits so he can keep an eye on Nash the entire time. He apparently seemed okay spending the day without him, however. Small steps.

"He needs a family," says Nash, sitting on a stool with his back to the flames. "People who'll be gentle with him, you know? He's been through enough, watching everybody die and then getting pushed around by Porter and his men. You guys are busy with Sophie. But someone's going to turn up who'll be right for the job."

Dean thinks it over. "He seems happy with you. Are you sure you don't want to hang around?"

"That's not me. Families and communities and stuff like that."

"I didn't come from a good background either," says Dean. "My childhood was a fucking horror story. But you seem to be doing okay with all of this so far."

Nash's expression is constantly set to blank, like he has to keep his emotions locked down. And he has this deep rumble of a voice. "I get that you're happy as a pig in shit with your woman and your daughter. But me living like this…"

"Let me put it another way," says Dean, as easy as can be. "You really think there's only one asshole like Porter out there? That boy is going to need you for a long time to come. I get that it can be terrifying having people counting on you. Needing to show up for them when you're not sure you can. But all he's asking is that you try. And whether you do or not could very well be the difference between life or death for him."

The way Nash's lips flatline. He is not happy. Not about any of this.

"Sophie just yawned so wide I could see her tonsils," I say, sensing it might be time to end the conversation. "We should get her home to bed."

Dean rises and offers me his hand. We say our good nights and gather our child and head on out. I didn't see Dean becoming such great parent material. Being a girl dad. What he said about showing up is the simple truth, however. He just keeps on keeping on. I hate how he was hurt as a child. The thought honestly makes me stabby.

He catches me giving him side-eye and says, "I'm okay."

"You'd tell me if you weren't, right?"

"Yeah. I'd tell you."

"If you ever want to talk about your childhood and things like that, I'm here, okay?"

"One day I'll tell you all about growing up in foster care. Being smacked around and the cigarettes burns and everything," he says. "But right now, being here with you and Soph, I am easily the happiest I've ever been. I honestly never knew life could be anything like this. And I just want to enjoy that for a while and not dwell in the past, you know?"

"Makes sense."

I give him a smile and he returns the sentiment. This is nice. I like this. And I sincerely hope whoever hurt him died a particularly slow and painful death.

The moon is bright enough to light our walk home. Sophie wanders on ahead while Dean walks beside me. Things don't feel all that different between us on the surface. Seems like he's letting me set the pace out in public. We usually hang out together at these things anyway. No need for me to cling to the man or anything. Though some handholding now and then might be nice. Maybe.

"You two are being weird," says Sophie. Like it's nothing personal, she's just making conversation.

Dean pauses. "In what way?"

"All of the smiling at each other. It's so weird."

"Were we doing that?" I ask. "I didn't notice."

"Hazel noticed," says Sophie.

Dean winces. "Yeah?"

"You were doing it at breakfast, too," she says. "Smiling at each other."

"Is that strange?" he asks. "Us smiling?"

Sophie makes a humming noise. "Not Astrid so much."

I nod. "She has a point. Your natural resting face does tend to be a frown."

"I don't have a resting frown face," he says, frowning. "That's not a thing. You just made that up."

"You're doing it right now." I point to his face and he snaps sharp teeth at my fingers, making me laugh. "It's right there."

"Oh my God," moans Sophie. The child is so dismayed by our behavior. "You're doing it again. You two are being so weird. Is it always going to be like this now?"

Dean stops fooling around and stands tall. "I'm sorry, Soph. Let's talk about this seriously for a minute. You know you can always ask us anything. We know things changing can be upsetting or confusing at times."

The child wrinkles her nose at him but says nothing.

"I also know you saw me coming out of Astrid's room this morning. And I will be sleeping in there with her from now on, okay?"

"Gross, Dean! I know how babies are made and where they come from! You don't need to tell me!" Such an immense expression of horror and disdain on her sweet little face. She turns and bolts for the house, leaving us in her dust. Where, according to her, we no doubt belong.

"I thought that actually went quite well," I say.

He grunts.

"You were very brave."

"Thanks." He takes a deep breath. "Fuck me. Parenthood."

I laugh quietly.

"So, we're gross apparently."

"This is awkward," I answer. "I think she only meant you."

"Really?"

"Yeah."

"*Shit*. Just between you and me, I am not actually sure how babies are made," he says. "Don't suppose you could give me a tutorial or something? I find hands-on teaching works best for me."

"No can do. I am helping with the watch for a couple of hours. And you need to get in there and make sure she remembers to brush her teeth before bed."

He presses a kiss against my cheek. It's as quick as can be, with no time for me to react or return the sentiment. The man is there and gone in an instant. "Dental duty it is," he says. "Be safe. I have watch from three a.m., so I'll see you in the morning."

SUNDAY

Wet weather makes for good cover. Nash and Dean head south to sneak up on Porter. Watch his camp for a while and see what's going on in the vicinity. While Naomi and I take the opportunity to check out some nearby farms. According to the books, citrus, avocadoes, and asparagus could well be out there ready to harvest. More real live fresh food would be amazing. Fingers crossed. And some chickens or goats would make my day. We really need to build a coop and pens for them first, though. Otherwise, we're just inviting chaos. Or more chaos.

Dean isn't happy about me heading out without him. The frown appears in full force. But we both have things to do. Life post-apocalypse waits for no one.

Our hopes or dreams for the farms are far and away exceeded from the start. Cows are roaming freely at the first ranch. The doors to the barn have been left open and with a pond on the property, they're living their best human-free life, so far as we can tell. Most of the farms in the area were organic and followed a sustainable philosophy. This seems to mean the animals have survived better than expected on their own. They weren't left in a cage due to sad and sorry circumstances.

Something has been preying on the chickens and other smaller animals at some of the properties, though. Wolves or coyotes or dogs gone wild. It could be any or all three. We put out extra food and water for the animals where we can. But on the whole, they seem to be nonplussed by the return of people into their existence. And honestly, who can blame them?

As for crops, we find some citrus. No one is going to die of scurvy. We mark on a map of the local area where apple orchards are to check later in the year. The farms also tend to trade in other useful items. Jerky, olive oil, and preserves, for starters. One farm we find has a bunch of strawberry plants in pots about to start fruiting. And another has blueberry and blackberry bushes ready to go into the ground. Most of them have died due to lack of water. I think I can save some of them, though.

By midday, we've hit five places. Which means it's time for us to go shopping in a cool small town to the north of Santa Rosa. Just for fun. Nash said Porter's people didn't go this far, so we should be safe. Though we're absolutely going to be as careful as possible. No idea what Cody the Creep was on about with saying towns up this way had been burned to the ground. Because the one we visit seems fine as can be.

"Pedro's dick does this thing…" says Naomi, gesturing with her finger. Not sure she should be making lewd finger gestures while driving, but here we are.

"I didn't know we were this close. That we like talked about this sort of stuff."

"Shut up." She laughs. "It like hits to the left sort of. Just amazing."

"Okay."

Naomi gives me all of the side-eye in all of the land and says, "So you and Dean finally did it. Congratulations."

"Thanks."

"I could tell because of your behavior, by the way. His hasn't changed in the least. Which is kind of comforting when you think about it. He's always been all about you. The man is obsessed."

"What do you mean? How have I been behaving differently?"

Her grin is so wide. "You watch him differently now. I mean, you always kept an eye on him. And you definitely appreciated the view no matter how deep in self-denial you were about it. But now you watch him like you want to write him bad poetry.

Compare his eyes to the stars and his dick to something suitably phallic and momentous. Nothing is coming to mind for me right now."

"The Leaning Tower of Pisa?"

She makes a choked sort of noise. "Sure. Why not."

"You're the one who introduced the concept of leaning dicks into the conversation." I smile. "Am I really that obvious?"

"Oh yeah," she says. "Everybody knows. Besides Charlie and the twins. But you know…their brains haven't fully developed yet."

"Huh. Sophie told us last night that we're gross and weird and she knows where babies come from."

Naomi sighs. "I mean, at least you don't have to start that conversation from scratch…"

"My thoughts exactly."

"Do you think Avan knows how to do an epidural?" she asks.

The way my stomach falls through the floor. Or maybe it's my uterus. "Shit. That's a very good question."

"He's been studying all of these textbooks, trying to upgrade his knowledge to doctor level," says Naomi. "Teaching Charlie how to become a paramedic as well."

"Good idea. We all need to learn what we can. I want to start doing some research on what contraception methods are available to us when the expiration dates on medicines and condoms and things like that are up."

"We're sure as fuck not going back to the rhythm method, because it does not work," says Naomi.

Our speed drops as we approach the town center and pull into a laneway. Everything seems quiet and still. We both have our guns on our hips. I am also carrying a lightened version of my backpack just in case. Going anywhere without some basic supplies and a first-aid kit these days is just silly.

There's no conversation while we make our way, keeping to the sides of buildings, trying to stay undercover. Out of the rain and out of view of anyone watching. The rain has lightened to little more than a shower, but another storm is coming. We crouch at the corner of a wine-tasting room. Across the street, from what I can see, is a yoga studio, an ice-cream parlor, a barber shop, a bakery, a chocolate company, and a restaurant. And on this side is a bookshop, a boutique, a toy store, an art gallery, and a cocktail bar.

However, Main Street goes on for several more blocks. Only the bar and a drugstore farther along seem to have been broken into. This place probably slapped back in days of yore. Signs advertise a street party with food trucks and live music. The date for which has already come and gone.

"Boutique, bookshop, chocolate place for starters?" whispers Naomi.

"Sounds good. And we definitely have to hit the toy store before we head home."

She nods.

However, we stay in place and watch a while longer. Everything seems normal. Nothing is out of place. There are some vehicles parked to the side and one left in the middle of the street down from us. The driver's door is standing open and a body is lying on the ground. From this distance, the decay seems about right for a death from the virus. I can't see any signs of violence.

Thunder crashes in the distance, and we both jump.

Naomi shakes her head. "Come on."

We head toward the boutique. When the door doesn't open, I pull the pry-bar tool thing out of my backpack, place it against the door, and look up. As soon as lightning makes a jagged path across the sky, I break the glass and thunder covers the noise for us. Hooray for Mother Nature.

Inside, there's a wide selection of denim, soft cotton tees, vintage boots, long flowy dresses, silver jewelry, and more. And we are not mad. Taking some time for pretty things is fun. Strange to think there'll be no more new fashion for a while. Whatever was in style when the world ended is what we'll be wearing for the foreseeable future. Along with the clothes hanging in people's closets. Damp and decay will decrease the amount over time, but some will survive to be worn another day.

It's been weeks since I shared a selfie or liked or commented. All of the things integral to everyday life have disappeared. The woman in the mirror has some color on her face from the sun. My hair is definitely wilder without the salon visits. But I am still me.

I find a straw cowboy hat for gardening, days-of-the-week underwear that I don't know how I have lived without, and a navy-and-white-striped ringer tee. And that's just for starters. Some warmer wear for when I'm on watch at night also seems smart, and a black silk-and-lace camisole top, because why not?

Guess I should leave room for books, chocolate, and toys. But it's hard to stop when it's free and you've basically been living in the same pair of jeans for a month. It would also be good not to have to do laundry as often. Handwashing everything takes time. Maybe another bag is the answer. Naomi is likewise busy loading up with goodies.

"Are you ready for the bookshop?" I ask, testing the weight of my backpack. Taking a load back to the truck is not out of the question.

Which is when we hear it…the sound of a baby crying.

Both of us hunker down and listen. And a male voice out on the street says, "Come on out here now. You three ladies don't want to be trying to make it on your own. Especially not with a kid. It's dangerous these days. All sorts of people are running around and hurting girls like you."

We crawl toward the front window. Two men are standing out in the street in the soft falling rain like they're in a movie. Guess they're the dramatic type. All we can see are their backs. But they're both holding pistols at their sides. And while they're not pointing them at anyone just yet, it doesn't seem like it would take much. Their stance is wired and ready to go. I do not trust them at all.

The group that they're talking to are standing outside one of the shops up from us, out of our range of view. A nervous-sounding woman says, "We're doing fine on our own."

"Come and see our place down at Sonoma," says the man doing all of the talking. "I promise you're going to love it."

It all sounds so horribly fucking familiar. What he's saying and the way they're standing and everything. Porter must give these guys a script or something.

"We're not going to take no for an answer," says the man, gesturing with his pistol. "Time for you to put that knife of yours down, honey. Now. None of us want things to become unpleasant here. But they will if you don't do as you're told."

And fuck this asshole. No way can we stay safe in hiding and let these women be taken.

Naomi and I share a look and head toward the shop door. It's like my blood has turned to ice. But I don't stop moving, slow and steady. Keeping low, we open the door. The sound of glass breaking beneath our boots is covered by the noise of the rain.

"Porter might even let you keep the baby," says the man. "I don't know. It really isn't so bad back at camp once you learn your place."

Crouched on the concrete sidewalk with one knee down for balance, I draw my pistol. His back makes for a nice solid target.

One of the women standing a few shops away notices our appearance. And the man who isn't talking begins to turn our way to see what's garnered her attention.

My pistol kicks hard in my hands.

The man who did all the talking makes a noise like all of the air just got shoved out of him. I fire again, and he falls to his knees before face-planting on asphalt.

It all happens so fast.

Meanwhile, the other guy is raising his gun in our direction. Naomi fires once, twice, and misses. Her target isn't as wide and static as mine. And the guy gets a shot off, though his aim isn't great. Something flies past my face, however. The heat of it leaving a line of fire on my forehead.

Naomi's third shot takes him smack between the eyes. He stumbles back a step before falling down.

And the three women with the baby are just standing there staring at us in horror and surprise. Which is fair enough. But we did it. We stopped the assholes from hurting these people.

From the end of the block comes the roar of an engine as an oversized SUV speeds away.

Shit. There were three of them, apparently. And the spare

is going to race straight to Porter and tell him what happened here. He already had a description of Naomi and me. Though, we *are* wet, and the weather is shit. No idea if he got a good look at us or not.

The three women are still just standing there staring at us. One is busy trying to pacify the poor baby. Our weapons obviously startled the little one. And those two freshly dead bodies on the ground sure are something to behold.

Naomi and I killed two people. Not what I thought would happen today, but here we are and there they are, and yeah.

Also, my head hurts and blood seems to be sliding down the side of my face. It's getting in my eye and everything.

Naomi turns to me with wide eyes. "Oh, fuck."

"I'm okay," I say, and vomit up the protein bar I had for lunch onto the pavement.

CHAPTER SIXTEEN

SUNDAY

"WHERE THE FUCK IS MY WIFE?" ASKS DEAN. "GET out of the way!"

Charlie jumps aside and my significant post-apocalypse other enters the room set aside for all things medical. His dark brows are drawn down and his mouth is a straight pissed-off line. I don't think I've ever seen the man so angry. Just fucking furious. Not to objectify him, but he sure is something when he's in a bad mood. It's the whole clenched-jaw and raging-eyes thing. Makes me want to climb him like a tree.

Night fell a few hours ago. But we took our time coming back to town to make sure we weren't followed. It seemed unlikely with the way the SUV tore off into the sunset. Best to be sure, however. The three women also wanted to be certain they weren't trading one type of tyranny for another. Now I am finally getting my head wound tended. Imagine almost having a bullet to the brain. Talk about close calls.

Sophie is hot on his heels through the door. "Dean, you didn't say please. And you're not supposed to use the F word."

"Please and sorry."

"Thank you for bringing him in, Nurse Sophie," says Avan. "Could you and Nurse Hazel please check on everyone in the kitchen for me? Make sure they're comfortable and have everything that they need?"

"Yes," says Sophie, and off she goes.

Just in time to miss the profoundly felt "Fuck me" from Dean.

"I know there's a lot of blood on her," says Avan. "But head wounds bleed a lot."

"How bad is it?" asks Dean. The idea that someone would hurt me has hit him hard. It's like his voice has dropped a full register. He's just so weighed down by all of the rage. "Are you in much pain?"

Avan, however, is unimpressed with the display of alpha male. He continues cleaning and closing the wound on my forehead. "I gave her something to take the edge off."

"Those small pills slap," I say with a smile.

"They do, huh?" asks Dean.

"I'm going to have a cool scar like a pirate."

With hands on hips, Dean sighs heartily. "Great."

"This bandage needs to stay dry," says Avan.

Dean just nods.

"What a day," I say. "You know, I would love a beer."

"Do not give her beer or any other form of alcohol," says Avan, taping gauze or something down over the wound. "Take her home, clean her up, and get her to bed."

"Got it," says Dean.

"We can negotiate on the beer, though, right?" I ask with my most endearing smile. "I really did have a day."

"No," say both Avan and Dean.

"Well, that's harsh."

Reema appears in the doorway. "Why doesn't Sophie have a sleepover with Hazel tonight? Let you concentrate on this one."

"That would be great. Thank you," says Dean.

He bundles me up in his leather jacket and we say good night to one and all. There'll be time for meeting the three new members of our community later. When he isn't having a meltdown over my head wound. Sophie and Hazel are busy oohing and aahing at the baby. To be fair, the baby is only a week old and super cute.

Which reminds me. "I pet a baby goat today. It was so soft and cute."

He gives me a look.

"What?" I ask. "Are you still in your feelings about me getting shot?"

"I am, funnily enough."

The new people are gathered at a table eating minestrone with Natalia and Naomi. It's going to be a while before they feel safe and sound. Given what they went through today, this makes sense.

"Good night, Nurse Sophie and Nurse Hazel," I say to the girls.

Nurse Sophie waggles a finger at me. "You should be resting in bed."

"She's such a hard-ass," I say to Dean, when we're outside in the still night air. "When are you on watch tonight?"

"Just watching you."

"I am okay. Really."

He does not seem convinced. And his arm is around my back, holding my elbow like I need steadying or something. Which I don't think I do, but whatever. When I tip my head back to see the stars, however, the world turns in dizzy circles. Maybe he's right about me needing a certain amount of monitoring. But like only a little.

As soon as we get home, I head for the bathroom and brush my teeth. No amount of mints made them feel clean after puking.

"Darling, are you going to tell me how you managed to take a bullet to the head?" he asks, watching me from the doorway.

"You haven't called me darling before. There's a testy edge to the endearment I don't trust."

"Is there?"

"You love me," I say, pointing my finger at him. "Say it, Dean. I think you need the reminder."

"I remember just fine. How did you get shot?"

"It only grazed me. Just like oh so vaguely winged me as it went on its way, you know?"

He gives me a look and waits not so patiently.

"Right. How it happened." I pour a cup of drinking water to rinse my mouth and toothbrush. "We went to the farms and that was all good. That's where the baby animals were. I am going to need your help building, um, chicken and goat houses too, or whatever they're called, by the way. Wouldn't it be great to have fresh eggs and milk? And then Naomi and I decided to do some shopping in a cool small town to the north. I found days-of-the-week underwear, isn't that fantastic?"

"Keep going," he says.

"The town was meant to be outside of where Porter usually sends his people." I hand him the leather jacket and toe off my socks and boots. And I almost tip over at one point, making him step forward to steady me. Oops. Next go the crusty tee and jeans. Dried bloodstains ahoy. The top can go into the compost or something. No way am I getting those marks out. My bra and underwear stay on for now. "But there were some there."

"Did they see you?"

"No."

"You couldn't have stayed safe out of sight?" he asks in a growl.

There are a couple of buckets of water in the bathroom for emergencies such as these. I grab a cloth and a bar of soap and start in on the mess that is me. However, he takes the cloth from me and carefully gets to work.

"Damn that water's cold. You know what would have happened to those women," I say. "What they would have done to them."

His mouth opens to argue, but no.

"They had their back to us," I say. "We were in a good position."

"Astrid—"

"Those assholes threatened a *baby*, Dean. They actually inferred that Porter might not let the mother keep her child."

He squeezes his eyelids shut tight for a moment. Then he starts carefully washing the dried blood from my face and neck. My shoulder, arm, and chest. Neither of us talks for a while. High as a kite as I am, I still know he needs time to process.

The water in the first bucket is soon the color of rust. With help, I wash my hair leaning over the edge of the bathtub, holding a towel to the bandage keeps it dry. Then I'm wrapped in a large plush towel. Dean sits on the bed, and I sit at his feet as he carefully brushes my hair.

"I don't feel as bad as I thought I would after killing someone," I say, resting my elbow on his denim-clad knee. "This worries me."

"Like you said, he threatened the life of a child. That's a whole new level of asshole."

"Yeah. I puked on the sidewalk. But I don't know if that was more from the shock of getting shot or what."

He just grunts. Like I know what the noise means. Each section of my hair is carefully lifted and worked over with the brush in his hand. The man would have made a hell of a maid.

"There's always this impossible weight when a character kills for the first time in books and movies. Like a burden that they assume. The cost of dealing in life and death," I say. "But I'm not feeling it. I get that deciding to kill someone is big. It doesn't seem like anyone should have the power of life and death. But there's no doubt in me that I made the right choice today. Does that make me a bad person or a decisive one or what?"

"Depends." He pauses to crack his neck. "Got the urge to go out and start killing people indiscriminately?"

"No."

"Would you kill someone for annoying you or something stupid?"

"I know I've threatened *you* a time or two…"

His chuckle hits me straight between the hips.

I wrap my arms around his legs and lean my cheek against his knee. Head wounds make me demonstrative, apparently. He's so big and warm, and he smells so good. And I may not be tearing myself in two over ending the lackey, but it doesn't mean I am not in need of comfort.

Here's the thing: within the privacy of my own skull, I can admit Dean has become my person. Not exactly sure what the job title "person" entails at this point in time. However, it's important and multilayered and detail-oriented and stuff. Very him-specific. I should probably just keep it to myself for now.

Which is why I open my mouth and say, "You're my person."

"I'm your person?"

"Oops. Didn't mean to say that out loud."

He pauses. "How high are you right now?"

"Yeah. Sort of." So many thoughts spinning around inside my mind. "I always wanted a person. It's just a game of luck, right? There are a lot of people out there. Or there *were* a lot of people out there. What are the chances that you meet the right person for you, though? Not good."

"Define the right person."

I shrug. "No can do. You just know that they're right."

"Okay," he says, sounding mildly freaked out for some reason.

"What's with the tone of voice?"

"Nothing. Just not used to not having to talk you into us.

This is a whole new level, even above having sex and sleeping together."

"Oh."

"Also not sure anyone has ever known me well enough to call me their person before."

I blow a raspberry. "You've hardly told me any of your stories."

"And you've hardly told me any of yours," he returns. "But we'll get around to it."

"I know you."

He laughs softly. "That's my point. We already know what each other is capable of. Who needs the rest?"

"Yeah," I say. "I wouldn't kill anyone who didn't need killing."

"That makes me feel so much better."

"Shut up. What I mean is, I'd be happy to never have to do it again. To never be in that position." I hold on to him tighter. "Say the thing."

"What thing?"

"You know what thing."

"But you just told me to shut up. So how can I say the thing?" he asks. "Besides which, need I remind you that the last time I said it, you were very unhappy at me. And in case you haven't noticed, that is the opposite of how I like you to be."

And enough of his bullshit. Seriously. Seems I was right the first time. He should stop talking. I shrug off the towel and rise up on my knees, all the better to turn and face him.

He takes one look at my face and says, "You're supposed

to be resting. 'Get her home, get her cleaned up, and get her to bed' were the orders."

"And here we are on the bed. I'll have you know, I am excellent at following orders."

"You're the worst at being told what to do. Avan didn't mean 'bed' like this, and you know it."

For all of his fine words, Dean doesn't fight me when I push him back onto the bed. Nope. His back meets the mattress without much of a fuss at all. I undo the buckle on his belt and he watches me all the while. As conflicted as he might be about going against medical orders, he doesn't make any move to slow things down or stop my hands. I can't remember the last time I undressed someone. Though I am thoroughly enjoying this experience.

It's like each time I touch him, I give him more of myself and take more of him for me. The button on his jeans and then the zipper. I push up his tee to expose more of his body. Such a handsome bastard. Naomi was right about me wanting to write him bad poetry. His beauty outshines the sparkling night sky. Yeah. Emphasis on the "bad" in bad poetry.

He's wearing another pair of dark gray boxer briefs. I slide the palms of my hands over his stomach. Just reveling in touching his skin, so hot and smooth. He's so very alive and vital to me in ways I am still trying to understand.

There's a treasure trail of dark hair leading down from his belly button. I grab the waistband of his underwear and his jeans and shuffle them down some. Give myself room to work.

"Fine. Whatever," he says. "Be irresponsible. Disregard medical advice and distract yourself with my dick. See if I care."

I just give him an amused glance. "You called me your wife again."

Nothing from him.

Seems as if his cock is thicker and longer this time than the last. Not sure how he's doing that. Man magic or something. But the veins are engorged and almost angry looking. And raised up on his elbows, Dean watches what I am doing with such interest. With so much hunger in his gaze.

I crouch beside him on the bed and wrap my fingers around his hardening cock. He has a salty, musky taste. And the noise he makes when I drag my tongue over the wide head is so very good. I am going to be hearing it in my dreams forever.

I tighten my fist around him. It's hard to say what he prefers more: me sucking on the head of his cock, or tracing the crown with the tip of my tongue. We both love me teasing him and taking him deep. However, his size presents certain limits. When he's good and hard, I stop and give him a smile.

"Is there something you want to say to me?" I ask.

"Why did you stop, you evil harpy?"

I give his cock another squeeze. "Try again, Dean."

"I love you, baby. You're my whole fucking world."

"Better."

And I slip off my underwear. Taking him in is my reward for surviving such an incredibly shitty day. Next, I undo the bra and his hands are right there, taking the weight of my breasts with eager fingers. Pinching and rolling my nipples. Making the need reach higher.

He rises up and grabs me by the back of the neck, bringing my mouth to his for the sweetest of kisses. For someone of his size, he can be so very gentle. But this is trust. I trust him with everything. And the thought doesn't even surprise me anymore.

He really is gorgeous when we're fucking. His cheekbones are stark and his mouth is wet and swollen. I love how dark his gaze goes. The thickness of him stretching me. How perfect the friction from his hard-on is, sliding in and out of my body. I mean to take it slow and make it last, but it doesn't work. *More, now, yes*, are the only words in me. There's no room for anything else. It's just him and me and this.

His hands grip my thighs tight, urging me to ride him faster, harder. Then one hand dips between my legs and the pad of his thumb teases over my clit. I am undone so damn quickly. It's like pure sensation tearing through me. Every nerve in me is set aflame.

I come, clenching hard on him, holding him deep. His hips kick beneath me, and his arms come around me. I am held tight against his chest. We're a sweaty post-sex mess. You have to respect the sacredness of the moment. Nothing is said for a while as we both come down and catch our breath.

"How's your head?" he asks finally.

"Still there."

He stuffs one hand beneath his head and presses the other palm against my back. Just holding me to him. "I really do love you. And you *are* the whole fucking world to me," he says. "So please understand that I am going to be gluing myself to your ass for a while because you scared the absolute shit out of me tonight."

I raise my head and set my chin on his chest. "Dean…"

"You got shot."

"It barely grazed me. My cool pirate scar isn't even going to be that big. Don't you think you're maybe overreacting?"

"No. This is me being reasonable, baby."

With a heartfelt sigh, I dismount the man and deliver a parting kiss to his lips. "I think you'll find that this is in fact you needing a good night's sleep, and you'll feel much better about it in the morning."

MONDAY

He does not, in fact, feel much better about it in the morning.

The day starts with a town meeting in the bed-and-breakfast. It's not like Dean and I didn't tend to hang out together. But it was never a *thing* before.

Now, don't think I play favorites with the furniture. There is, however, an armchair that offers a spectacular sitting experience. Just delivers a perfect balance between soft and firm that so few seats are willing to offer. Seeing it was empty, I, of course, made straight for this singular delight of a chair.

"Why don't we sit on that sofa," he says, taking a sip from his cup of coffee.

"You go. I'm good here."

So he sits himself on the arm of my chair. Hovering over me.

"Has everyone met Jodi and Vivianna?" asks Reema, standing beside the fireplace. "Make sure you've taken a moment to introduce yourself. Amel couldn't be here because she's busy with the baby. They've moved into the house across the street, if anyone wants to stop by and say hi. Though knock softly. You don't want to wake anyone who might be sleeping."

Jodi is a white woman in her twenties with a cool bleached-blonde shag haircut. Vivianna is around the same age and has olive skin, long dark hair, and is drop-dead gorgeous. Proof at least some supermodels survived the virus. They sit close together, holding hands. Nice to hear our population has officially reached twenty-one.

"Wyatt and Jack are on watch, and Pedro and Nash have already headed out to keep an eye on Porter's camp," continues Reema. "Care to comment on what you saw there yesterday, Dean?"

"He chose well for his position. Access to the property is through a tall iron gate that is constantly monitored by two of his men. They communicate frequently with others via a two-way radio. There's a seven-or-so-foot-high brick wall surrounding the place," he says. "Guards walk the perimeter regularly, inside and out. We saw five vehicles head off in different directions with three men in each."

"One of which we assume Naomi and Astrid came across," says Leon, writing in a small notepad.

Dean frowns. "Yeah. On the property, there are three main buildings. The first one has the guesthouse, event center, and offices. The second is the cellar where the wine was made, stored, and sold. And the third is a barn."

"How many people do you think are there?" asks Reema. "Nash previously said around thirty. Are we still looking at that figure?"

"No," says Dean. "We counted close to forty."

"Shit," someone swears.

Leon taps a pen against his lips. "We still need more people."

"Don't you think you're maybe rushing things? I mean, those guys were creepy as fuck," says Jodi. "Guess I'm still trying to get my head around everything that happened yesterday. But did you actually see any women being abused at this camp?"

"Not any live ones." Dean's dark brows draw tight together. "They brought out a body and put it in the back of a pickup. Just dumped her down the road."

Jodi's face is white as can be, and I don't blame her.

Trisha clears her throat. "Could you tell how…"

"She'd been beaten," says Dean. "It was hard to tell much from the damage, but she seemed young. I doubt she was older than twenty. We wanted to bury her, but…"

I place my palm on his jean-clad thigh, and he covers it with his hand. That he had to see such a thing. My heart hurts for him.

"And he has forty people who want to do this sort of shit," I say. "I never really believed so many people hated women."

Reema sighs. "They're pitiful, small, insecure assholes who only feel tall when their boot is on someone's neck or when vile deeds are being done to another."

"They need killing," says Naomi.

Dean's gaze is cold and hard. "Yes, they do."

And no one disagrees.

CHAPTER SEVENTEEN

MONDAY

DEAN MEANT IT ABOUT GLUING HIMSELF TO ME. No hyperbole. None at all. I may believe his claims of not stalking me back in Portland, but he's sure as fuck making up for it now. Seeing the murdered woman yesterday can't help but have affected him. And me almost getting shot in the head is obviously not a soothing thought for him. He just needs some time.

I have the children after the meeting. The plan is to get the strawberry and blueberry plants from yesterday into the ground. But first we hit up the library for some fresh reading material. I need to learn about chickens and goats. While the children search for more interesting and varied topics, such as sharks and castles.

"There's a moat around half of the town," Hazel tells me.

Bowie nods. "We just need to figure out how to put sharks in it."

"I like this idea," says Dean.

"They won't be able to make us take baths in the cold water if there are sharks in there," adds Bowie.

Dean thinks it over and nods. "Very true."

The children have nominated their pack animal for the day. Dean's job is to carry the market bag, into which goes all of their books, along with anything else they find of interest. Nurse Sophie tries to take a book on bullet wounds, all the better to care for me in my time of need. But given the graphic nature of the photos, we talk her out of that one. Thank goodness. My head is not amazing. However, painkillers are keeping it under control.

This is about the time when Sophie remembers the contents of her pockets. We're sitting outside on the courthouse steps. Yesterday's clouds have cleared to a perfect blue sky. Good weather for sitting outside and getting into some trail mix.

"Are you going to eat all of the candy out of mine?" asks Dean with a frown.

I nod. "Yes."

He grunts.

"I almost forgot. We found these," says Sophie, spilling out shining rings onto the step between us. "Natalia had some at her house, and I told Leon what we were doing and he took us around to a few places."

"Whoa," I say. "Those are real. How big is that diamond?"

"What are they for, Soph?" asks Dean, who is not a soulless consumer in love with shiny things like me.

Her expression is pained. Like it's so hard for her to have to deal with such dim-witted fools. "You keep calling her your wife, but you don't wear rings! You have to wear rings if you're married!"

"We do, don't we? What a great idea." Dean sorts through the jewelry. He tries on a couple of gold bands, but they're too small. Then he picks up a simple thick silver band and slips it on his ring finger. "This one works."

And I have a whole lot of nothing to say about any of this. Because those are absolutely real engagement and wedding rings spread out on the step. The man is marrying himself—to me. Like the first time he told me he loves me, this moment has me in a chokehold. It's meant to be big. One you remember for the rest of your life.

"Astrid has to put it on you," instructs Sophie.

Hazel nods. "It's how it happens in the movies. The other person puts it on your finger."

Bowie is too busy eating trail mix to express an opinion.

Dean takes off the ring and holds it to me with a hint of a smile curving his lips. "Would you do me the honor?"

"I don't know." I peer down my nose at him and the ring and shove some more candy into my mouth. "It's not like you've wooed me or asked me properly or anything."

"How do you define 'wooed'?" he asks. "Because I feel like I exclusively focused on you and your safety and happiness."

"You exclusively focused on my happiness?"

"On your long-term happiness," he says. "You have to be alive to be happy, right?"

The funny fucker knows I am not saying anything about a cage in front of the children. I take the ring and turn it around and around. "You didn't even ask me out until the world was ending. And then it was entirely on your own terms."

He ignores me and carries on with his nonsense, saying, "For better or for worse, in sickness and in health—"

"Isn't 'to love and to cherish' meant to go in there somewhere?"

"Till death do us part—"

"Is that why you waited outside the bathroom this morning while I used the facilities? Are you telling me I am not going to have a moment's peace until one of us joins the dearly departed?" I ask. "Because I'm not sure how I feel about that."

The children's heads turn back and forth between us like it's a sports match. Not sure we're really modeling a healthy relationship.

"You're smiling," he says with a grin. "You don't hate the idea of forever with me."

"I have issues, clearly. But this is not a wedding. This is just me going along with this for now so you don't lose all credibility in front of the children." The ring slides down his finger without too much resistance. Hate to say it, but it looks good on the man. And I don't hate how I was the one who put it on him. "Don't let it be said I didn't give you pretty trinkets."

"You're the prettiest. Nothing else matters and you know it. And I'll be wrapped around your finger until the day I die."

One day, I will learn how not to smile when he says such cheesy things. When the dairy is so blatantly in your face. But that day is not today. "I guess that's as official as it gets."

"We should ask Reema to marry us sometime. She's official. Then you can wear the dress, and we can have a party."

"And we'll be the flower people!" shouts Sophie with glee.

"Yes!" screams Hazel. Truly the child has a remarkable set of lungs on her and much passion for life.

The solemn moment is broken by the appearance of a small black canine. No idea what breed it is. Some sort of lapdog, by the look. However, it sees the children and wags its muddy, tangled tail with glee. And the sentiment is most definitely returned in kind.

Soph's face is filled with delight. "It's a puppy!"

"No," says Dean with dawning horror. "That is not what I meant by a dog."

But no one is listening to him. Not even me.

"We're in Northern California," says Pedro on the two-way radio. "That's about as comfortable as we are narrowing down our location, given everything."

"Understandable," answers the person he's been talking to for the past half hour. "Any other pieces of information or areas outside of Sonoma you advise us to avoid?"

"The group numbers around forty and monitors an area of about an hour's radius, from what we've been able to tell."

"Got it. I appreciate the intel. Our group isn't that large, though it *is* sizeable. Hopefully there are enough of us to warn them off."

Sophie and Roger the dog are asleep in her bedroom. Honey the German shepherd gave Roger the lapdog of dubious heritage a dismissive sniff and then ignored him. However, Roger didn't seem much to mind. He gets away with sitting on the furniture and sleeping on a bed while Honey has to stay on the floor. It's easy to see who he believes is the true winner in this situation. And yes, Roger had a bath before coming inside the house. I don't want to know what the little dog had rolled in, but the stench was potent.

Nash and Pedro came back in the evening with much the same news Dean gave us at this morning's meeting. We would need to attack during the day when Porter's five vehicles go out to monitor the spots they've claimed as theirs. It's the only time our numbers come even close to theirs. We need more people, a foolproof plan, and we need to prepare.

With this in mind, George and the twins went shopping. They returned with a couple more military vehicles loaded with weapons, bulletproof vests, and various other supplies. Most of it from camps and blockades in towns north and west of us. Along with the military vehicles here already, they're parked at intervals throughout town, ready to go. Porter might still find us first. We need an escape plan.

Weapons are hidden in each of the houses. We practiced getting down low and getting to the nearest cover with the children. Reiterated gun safety to them and the general no-touching rule. Someone is usually keeping an eye on the children. Though having guns in the house still feels like trading one danger for another. There are also vehicles with full gas tanks and stocked with supplies ready to go on the other side of the creek. Just in case. I don't know how to defend a place like this. But with these preparations we hopefully have a chance, at least.

But back to the radio. Pedro, Naomi, Dean, and I are gathered in our living room. Porter used the radio to help draft dickheads. We're going to use it to warn anyone who's listening. And to hopefully meet some more people to boost our population.

"I don't suppose you're looking for somewhere to land?" asks Pedro.

"We've not quite finished our journey yet," says the man on the radio. He sounds maybe middle-aged. "I started in Grand Junction and headed west. More and more people joined along the way. Traveling seemed sort of cathartic amongst all of the chaos. But I'm honestly not sure what happens next. You're right about us needing to settle somewhere. And where we're going may not be best suited."

"There's a lot to consider," Pedro says. "Between putting the dead in the ground and collecting food stores and medicine, things have been busy here. Join us, and you have the benefit of our head start. Though as mentioned, we have unfortunately made ourselves an enemy."

"I appreciate the offer, and we'll definitely give it some thought," the man says. "This is a pilgrimage for me. My daughter passed early from the virus. She was only seventeen and had been planning on studying architecture. Just loved looking at interesting buildings that were environmentally conscious. It was her passion. She always wanted to see the ocean as well. I just never got around to taking her."

"Right," says Pedro in a gentle voice.

"Life gets so busy and all of the meaningless shit takes over. Anyway…there was this one place she talked about, and we should reach there tomorrow," he says. "Ask me after that."

"Will do. Good night and safe travels." Pedro turns off the radio with a disappointed sigh. "Guess we try again tomorrow."

"Or we could go meet them and ask in person," I say.

Naomi cocks her head. "You've figured out where they're going to be."

"Interesting, environmentally conscious buildings by the ocean, and the reception was strong, so they're probably kind of close, right?" I ask. "They're going to Sea Ranch."

TUESDAY

"It's not fair—I figured it out," I say.

"Their first impression of our group can't be a woman with a fresh bullet wound on her forehead, and you know it." Dean finishes his coffee and rinses out his mug in the soapy water in the sink. "And you've got a headache and should be resting. Not going off on adventures."

"I already took some Advil. I'll be fine in a minute."

"Great. What's on for today?" he asks, hands on hips. "You want to start giving me directions for building a chicken coop?"

"No. Not right now."

"Okay," he says. "What then?"

"I need you to go be somewhere else and give me some space."

"No. You have a head wound, and I am sticking close to you. What if you have a dizzy spell or something?"

"Listen to me very carefully, Dean," I say. "You not only didn't wake me up when you knew there was a town meeting happening, so I couldn't be part of the decision-making process around who would go to Sea Ranch and how things would be handled. But you waited until they'd left to wake me, just to make absolutely certain my ass was stuck at home."

He stares down at me with his lips a flat and final line. "There was never any chance of you going on that trip. None. You're wounded and need to rest. I stand by my decision."

"Oh yeah?" I hate the way my voice cracks. "Well, you can sleep beside it too. Because you're sure as shit not sleeping with me."

"That's not what we agreed."

"I never agreed to you treating me like a child and making decisions for me without consultation. Especially ones that you know damn well I would not be okay with."

His mouth snaps shut, and he says no more.

"Yeah," I say. "That's what I thought."

"All I said is that I can see his side." Leon sits beside Natalia on a blanket in the shade of an elm in our yard. He's smoking another one of those fancy cigars. "He's just trying to protect his girl. How is that so wrong?"

"Thank you, Leon," says Dean, from where he's measuring timber for the chicken coop nearby.

Natalia harrumphs. "His girl is a grown woman who can make her own choices."

Trisha makes a noise of agreement.

There's rain coming, making it perfect weather for gardening. Trisha and I are planting some of the seedlings and doing the weeding. Since Dean refuses to give me space, I am sticking to outdoor areas where ignoring him is easiest. Living in a community where people care about each other and want to be involved in each other's lives is great. Right up until you're having your first fight with your significant other and everyone is sticking their nose into same.

Therefore, I am ignoring Dean and this conversation. Because inviting Wolf Creek into our relationship sounds like a dreadful idea to me.

Back when we had televisions it might not have been such an issue. People could watch their soap operas or their dramas or catch the news. Get their fix of who's doing what and what's going on from the flat screen. Pedro and Naomi have been together for a few days already. They're old gossip. One of the twins lost a game of cards the other night and had to run buck naked through town, apparently. Also, Vivianna was a concert violinist and gave a performance on their front porch yesterday. But right now, the only entertainment in town is me and Dean.

"She could have been killed the other day," says Leon. "Of course he's worried about her."

Trisha sits back on her heels and fans her face with her ball cap. The day is warming up. "You can be worried about someone without taking away their agency. Love is having someone's back. Not smothering them in bubble wrap. What Dean did was disrespectful."

"He also told us she'd be okay with the meeting going ahead when he very much knew that was not the case," says Natalia.

Leon sighs. "He's in love. It's hard for a man not to want to protect the person he's given his heart to."

"This isn't about genitals or supposed gender norms,"

chides Trisha. "We *show* love. We don't enforce it. And a love that takes away your rights is not a love worth having."

Dean is frowning big time. I can see him out of the corner of my eye. I almost feel bad for him, having Natalia and Trisha on his case. Almost.

"He manipulated us and disrespected his wife," says Natalia. "He has some thinking to do."

As much as I've enjoyed watching Dean get a verbal spanking, enough already.

"I love you all," I say. "But I am going to have to ask you to stay out of my marriage."

Dean stares at me in shock. He's subtle about it, but I can tell. Guess it's the first time I've referred to what we have as a marriage. But it's the simple truth. I am here with him for the duration. No one else interests me. This tangled and complicated relationship is it for me. Me and him, sitting on the front porch of our house watching the sun set for the next forty or so years, sounds like heaven. Having him hovering and figuring out how we work together. It's all I want or need in this life he has given me.

He blinks and licks his lips and tells me, "They're right about everything. Natalia and Trisha, I mean."

"Fuck you," mumbles Leon. "See if I'm on your side next time, son."

"I am sorry. You have every right to make your own decisions. I got scared at the idea of you getting hurt again and panicked. I can't say it won't happen again because I'm not always exactly rational when it comes to you. But I'll try to keep my shit under control. Because hurting you…disrespecting or disappointing you…they're the last things I would ever want to do," he says. Talk about giving good grovel. "Do you forgive me?"

I grace him with a queenly nod. "I'll think about it."

He snorts.

There's a small chance I have issues with public nudity. When a sponge bath with a bucket of water doesn't appeal, I head for the creek. Many of the town's citizens go naked. Just let it all hang out. But I have a black swimsuit from the boutique in town. I mean, you never know who you might run into down there. Twilight is one of the prettiest times of the day. From the golden light of the last rays of sunshine to the silver mist of the coming night.

Pedro, Naomi, Nash, and Charlie haven't yet returned from Sea Ranch. Hopefully this means the new group are interested in joining us. The twins are currently on patrol and listening for any updates from Naomi. Dean has stopped hovering and is making dinner. Though if I take longer than a quarter of an hour at the creek, he said he would come looking. And the children are busy with sticker and sketch books at the bed-and-breakfast. They had a big day. Natalia has started teaching them Spanish and George gave them lessons in safely starting a fire and how to read a map.

The water temperature is best described as refreshing. As much as I tell myself it's warming up more every day, summer is still a while away. Avan checked my war wound and changed the dressing to a waterproof one. Throwing myself in is the best way. To get the shock of the cold water over and done with at once.

There's no underestimating the spluttering and carrying on

when I surface. One day soon we're going to be able to risk the noise and run generators. We will have hot water for showers and everything will be good again. I long for that day. Sophie and the other children don't seem to have any problems frolicking in the arctic water. But it steals the breath out of me.

Then, out of nowhere, a strong hand grabs a fistful of my hair from behind and a blade is pressed against my neck. "Well now," says the gravelly voice against my ear. "You're even prettier than I was told."

My shaking is partly from the cold water, but mostly from him as I say, "Let me guess—you must be Porter."

CHAPTER EIGHTEEN

TUESDAY

"THIS IS SUCH BAD TIMING," I SAY, AS HE WALKS US out of the creek and onto the grass.

More of his men appear from between the trees up and down the length of the waterway. Over a dozen of them. More are probably coming in on the road and around the creek bend, out of sight. But our people have to be catching this on the cameras. Surely.

"Why is that, honey?" asks Porter. He's a blocky middle-aged man with a squinty stare and an unattractive aura. Never actually described anyone as having such a thing before. But wow does he have one. Just ugly as sin.

"I only now convinced my husband that he doesn't need to follow me everywhere to keep me safe," I say.

Porter hisses through his teeth. "Shit."

"I know, right?"

"If it makes you feel any better, he's going to be the first person I kill when we get up there."

I give him a brilliant smile. "Makes perfect sense. It's not like your pencil dick could compare to his man meat, right?"

Someone snorts nearby, but hastily turns it into a cough. Coward.

Which is when Porter releases his hold on my hair and swaps the hand holding his knife. Then he punches me in the face. He has a solid right hook. On the off chance I survive the next while, I won't be using my left eye.

I stay crashed out on the ground, stunned for a minute. But getting hit in the face a second time isn't quite as shocking. Don't get me wrong; it's still not fun. However, I think I might be getting used to it now. Not something I thought would ever happen, but here we are. The whole left side of my face is throbbing. And I am too stubborn and mouthy to regret a single fucking thing.

Shouts and shots are heard from the town. Near the road with the blockade and over by the bed-and-breakfast, by the sounds of things. *Oh fuck.* That's where the children are. Not only is it a surprise attack, but we're outnumbered.

Porter zip-ties my wrists together in front of me and passes me off to one of his men. Some dude who tosses me over his shoulder in a fireman's pose. And we're off and running toward town. His shoulder digs deep into my stomach with each step. I do not recommend the experience.

Demand for me was never this high back in normal times. I am a little bemused at being so popular at the end of the world. No matter which way I twist and turn my hands, they remain bound. I don't know how to get out of this. I don't know how to help anyone.

"Hang back with her," orders Porter.

The one carrying me drops me onto the grass beside a house at the back of town. And I do mean drops. It takes me a minute to catch my breath. But I have obviously been designated useless and down for the count by this dick. Because he crouches and turns his back on me to keep an eye on the street and anyone trying to come hither to kill him. I think having to stay out of the fight and guard me has hurt his feelings. There's a whole lot of grumbling going on. Judging by what he's saying, it seems his workplace is toxic, and his input is being consistently either overlooked and or unappreciated.

Haven't we all been there at one time or another?

What I really love are gardeners. And the one who lived in this house had a thing for big old terra-cotta pots full of flowers. Unfortunately, the plants have died in this case. But no problem. The combined weight of the pot and soil should do the job just fine.

What I need is to be quick and quiet. Two things no one has ever accused me of being. However, no one threatened my family before. And the sound of gunfire can still be heard coming from various parts of town.

Meanwhile, this dick is still busy bitching. He doesn't even notice me creeping up on him with the big-ass pot. I bring the thing down on his skull with all of the wrath I have in me. And believe me, it is quite a lot.

He doesn't move. He doesn't speak. He doesn't breathe.

I only slightly cut my hand with the knife he carries on his belt. But to get the zip-ties off is worth it. I tie my hair back in a knot to get it out of the way. The dead guy had two pistols. No idea what they are or how many bullets are in the magazines. I need to do what I can to help. Now.

The fastest way is to cut through a couple of backyards. Some of the people in Wolf Creek were low-key on fences, and I, for one, really appreciate it. I know in stories they always say it's cowardly and wrong to shoot people in the back. But I've done it once before and only just attacked someone with a pot from behind. When you think about it, it's almost become my signature style.

No idea if it's adrenaline or getting punched in the face making my brain throb and my blood hammer behind my ears. My vision wavers, and no. *Shit.* I don't have time for this. Just because I almost also got shot in the head the other day. Human bodies are so faulty and frail. Honestly.

One group of the assholes have surrounded the bed-and-breakfast. Most of them are taking cover behind the vehicles we loaded up with fuel and weapons and stores and parked at regular spaces along the street. Our get-out-of-Dodge emergency vehicles. They're not using the weapons inside the vehicles, though, because they don't know they're there. We didn't just leave guns and ammunition in view.

Some of them are taking cover behind neighboring houses. The poor beautiful old bed-and-breakfast has been shot to shit. Glass windows shattered, and the house is being shredded. People had already started gathering there for dinner. Dean, Trisha, Leon, George, and Avan are returning fire. It must be just Jack and Wyatt holding off the assholes at the other end of town. There's a decent stock of pistols and rifles inside the house. But without help coming, they can't hold out forever. And I am one woman with limited training when it comes to this stuff.

Wait a minute… The assholes are hiding behind cars with full fuel tanks.

I remember the time on the highway when the dude in the speeding sports car hit the power pole and went up with a bang. Blowing things up seems an extreme reaction, but this is an extreme situation.

With my head low, I backtrack to the neighboring house. The one with the hot tub, funnily enough. My bare feet hurt for some reason, but I don't have time to sort out shoes. The twins went out yesterday with their grandfather to collect military equipment. And if anyone is going to hold on to something they shouldn't, it's going to be the twins. Bless those boys.

It doesn't even take me long to find the grenades. Because of course they're going to leave grenades in a fruit basket on the kitchen counter. Someone really needs to have a talk to Jack and Wyatt about safe storage of munitions. My hands are shaking so bad. There's every chance this is an awful idea. But it's also just about my *only* idea. Should we both survive this, Dean is going to lose his shit. Completely. Like it will be a miracle if I get to pee in peace for the rest of my life.

I grab the denim jacket off the back of a kitchen chair and do up the buttons. Grenades handily fit in each of the two front pockets. Then back out onto the street I go, trying to stay calm.

The shooting doesn't stop. Someone cackles like a mad thing. There comes a pained hollering from inside, and Trisha shouts, "George!"

No more delaying. There's no time like the present. Time for an agitator, and that would be me. Though maybe it should be disruptor. I don't know.

Three of Porter's men are behind the nearest vehicle. And they're not paying any attention to their six. Not looking my way or expecting any trouble. Nope. Which is how I'm able to pull the pin and roll the grenade underneath the car. My father would be so proud knowing the nights we went bowling when I was a child have finally come in handy.

And I can now safely say I have, in fact, run like my ass is on fire. It wasn't many steps before the ground heaved and buckled beneath my feet. Never in my life have I heard a boom so big. Just catastrophic. Like the whole world went bang and reality tore itself in two.

But I was the only one expecting it. Which meant while everyone was still trying to figure out what had happened, I could creep up on another vehicle and use the other grenade. Four of Porter's men are hiding behind this vehicle. Pin. Toss. Turn and run.

I made it to the neighbor's fence. This time the boom seemed even more explosive, if possible. I also think I'm losing my hearing. The world seems strangely muted for some reason. Blowing things up, however, seems to be working. Two grenades were a great start, but I can see now that more are needed. As soon as I find my feet I am heading back to the twin's place.

With my hearing being weird, no wonder Porter catches me by surprise. His fingers digging into my arm as he drags me to my feet and shoves the barrel of his gun against my head. His angry mouth is moving, but I have no idea what he's saying. Nothing complimentary about me, would be my guess. Can't really blame him for having hurt feelings about me blowing up his men, but then it was his people who started all of this. Hopefully the grenades gave the townsfolk a chance to level the playing field.

I'd rather not die now all things considered. However, there's no doubting I've done some of my best living in the last few weeks. My heart has doubled in size, and I've loved more than I knew I was capable of. If this is to be my ending, then it honestly doesn't seem like such a bad one to me. To give my life for my family and friends is actually a beautiful thing.

The shining point of Dean's thin long blade reflects the last of the sun's rays. It's really quite cinematic. How a flash of silver and gold cuts through the smoke and shadows.

In through the asshole's ear it goes, and all signs of life disappear from his eyes. And the same time this is happening, Dean grips the gun pointed at my temple and tosses it aside. Guess I am not dying today after all. My guardian angel still has my back and thank fuck for that.

Porter's body slumps to the ground, and good riddance. Makes it the perfect time for Naomi, Pedro, and Charlie to arrive with some new friends. Though the death of their beloved leader seems to have stolen the fire from the bulk of the invaders. Most of them just turn and run. Our returning friends get busy dealing with the rest of them.

"Are the children okay?" I ask.

He nods his head. Thank goodness. Dean is saying something. I can see his lips moving, but I can't hear much of anything.

"I think my hearing is wonky from the grenades. There's just this ringing sound." Not sure if I'm speaking normally or shouting. It honestly could be either. "But I blew those cars up! Did you see?"

He nods.

"It was amazing. Made a bit of a mess though. We should probably keep the kids inside for a while."

He reaches out with one of his big-ass hands and gently

examines my latest facial wound. And of course he's way more upset about it than I am.

"I said his pencil dick couldn't compare to your man meat." I shrug. "I know I said I wouldn't say things that made assholes want to punch me, but…"

His lips make the required shapes for "man meat."

"Oh, come on. You have to admit, it's kind of funny."

He shakes his head and wraps his arms around me, hanging on tight. And his lips are moving against my cheek. Not kissing me, but saying something over and over and over again.

"I know," I say or yell or whatever. "I love you too."

George sadly doesn't survive the attack. He took a bullet to the neck defending the children in the bed-and-breakfast. The man died a hero. Trisha and the twins are devastated by the loss. I can't imagine the pain of losing your partner of almost fifty years. They spent a lifetime together. For it to come to an end here, today, because of these assholes, makes me furious and sad.

Avan sutures a knife wound to Wyatt's ribs, digs a bullet out of Jodi's shoulder, and removes a wooden splinter from Leon's eye. As for me, I sit on a sofa in the living room at the bed-and-breakfast with a cold compress on my face and a couple of bandages on my feet and arms and back. Seems I stepped on some broken glass during my adventures and took some shrapnel from the grenade blasts. Nothing too bad, luckily. But I'll have a couple more pirate scars. Guess I didn't feel it at the time due to adrenaline. Reema gave me some sweats and socks to wear. There are occasions when pants just do feel necessary.

Sophie and the other children are gathered around me,

watching all of the activity. They seem sort of shell-shocked and dazed after everything, which makes sense. Roger the lapdog is comforting them some. And Charlie is kindly making them some freeze-dried mac and cheese. We gave them soda to drink to keep up their sugar levels. Surges in adrenaline can mess with it, apparently. They also just deserve nice things after the horrific day.

There are fifteen new people. And several of them seem very comfortable carrying weapons and seeing to business. We'll meet the bulk of them tomorrow. Right now, we're all still busy catching our breath and processing. But I am told there are four children with the group, which is wonderful.

As for the cleanup…all of the bad guys have run or are dead. Pedro is taking Honey around town to sniff out any lingering danger. Dean and Charlie boarded up the broken windows of the house. And tomorrow we're going down to Sonoma to kill any stragglers. They don't get to survive after the harm they've caused. We won't allow them to keep kidnapping and killing, or to restart Porter's kingdom elsewhere. Fuck no. Their stores will also come in handy.

Jack wanders over and shouts at me, "You blew up people with our grenades. Good work."

"Thank you. I really am sorry about your grandpa. He was a wonderful person."

He just nods. His eyes are red and his expression is strained. Grief is hard.

Wyatt joins us with three crystal glasses and hands me one. The amber liquor smells like whiskey. "To Grandpa and grenades," he says, raising his glass in toast.

Jack and I do likewise before drinking. *Oof.* Yeah. Now I know I am still alive. The alcohol burns the whole way down.

Dean walks in from outside and comes straight over to me. His gaze runs over me and Sophie, making sure we're okay. Then, since the sofa is full, he sits on the rug on the floor at my feet with his back against the bottom of the couch. He stretches his legs out in front of him and crosses them at the ankles and rests his elbow on my lap.

Something in me relaxes with him here. He feels like a missing part of me returned. As if some of my heart and brain and spirit were waiting for him to make it whole. Which sounds horribly codependent, but he doesn't make me weaker, and I know I would walk away if we were untenable. But we're not. We make each other better. This world is better with him.

I hand him the glass of whiskey, and he takes a sip.

"Are you supposed to be drinking?" he asks in a raised voice so I can hear.

"It's medicinal."

He shakes his head.

I hold the cold pack to my face with one hand and run the fingers of my spare hand through his dark hair. It's damp from the rain outside. He might be right about me giving him grays. There do seem to be a few extra in sight. But he's going to make one heck of a gray fox. Me getting him there is basically a community service. People should thank me. Those small wrinkles radiating out from his blue eyes and the lines upon his brow. Ogling him until the day I die sounds sublime.

"Going to have to fix the holes in these walls," he says in the same raised voice.

"I love you."

He turns his head to me and says, "Do me a favor and tell me that every day?"

"You got it." It feels wrong to be this happy on a day like this. But I am. And I am going to stay that way for a long time to come.

EPILOGUE

ONE MONTH LATER

Wolf Creek's first wedding takes place in the small park. The sky is blue, and the sun is shining. Reema, Naomi, and I had a great time hunting for dresses. Mine is a vintage-style white lace with flutter sleeves, a V neckline, and pearl buttons on the back leading to a flowing skirt with a short train. Dean is wearing a white button-down with black trousers and matching boots. It's as dressed up as he gets. And I know he has at least one gun on him somewhere.

We have trestle tables and chairs set out with daisies in small vases. With the chicken and goats providing eggs and milk, our food selection has expanded. However, Trisha has been teaching us about the delights of long-life butter and egg powder. On the menu is corn bread, grilled chicken, coleslaw, mac and cheese (the children insisted), and vanilla bean cupcakes. With the fridge working in the storage house, Dean even gets his ice-cold beer.

The thirty-something people who now live in town are gathered and Naomi has played our song on the guitar. "Wildflowers" by Tom Petty. Reema is ready to get us married. There is just one small problem. Our head flower person has taken offense at part of the proceedings and staged a revolt. She did this by climbing a tree with the wedding rings in the pocket of her dress.

Our third flower person, Bowie, then got bored and climbed a nearby tree too. Because more members of the wedding party up trees is exactly what this situation needed.

"But they have to kiss," says Hazel for the hundredth time. "It's what people do at weddings."

"No!" shouts Sophie. "Nobody wants to see that!"

Bowie points to the north. "Whoa. I think that's an eagle."

"Dude, get down here," says Nash, who went so far as to put on a clean pair of blue jeans and a navy button-down shirt for the occasion. He's settling into single parenthood surprisingly well. And Bowie is generally more relaxed and happier now, which is great. "Please."

Bowie sighs, as if he's very badly done by indeed. But he does start the climb back down.

As opposed to my child, who is busy tearing ribbons out of her hair. "And I am not wearing these."

"Okay," I say. Then whisper to my other half, "She chose them."

Dean just shrugs.

Bowie reaches the ground and Nash takes him and Hazel back to join the party. What a day. Seriously.

It should be noted that no one is actually upset about the delay. Our guests are all happily enjoying an ice-cold beverage. Alcoholic or otherwise, depending on their age and inclination. However, there are those who are sampling a spirit, wine, or beer who are starting to get somewhat rowdy. We knew this was going to be the party of the summer. Roger the lapdog is already asleep underneath a neighboring tree. He has a full stomach due to stealing a cupcake earlier.

I have managed to get Sophie to talk about her feelings a time or two. And I think she's mostly worried about things changing. Finding rings for us and having a party is fun. But us actually getting officially married might mean things are different at home. She already lost one home and is scared of losing another. Which is why she's now up a tree in protest over us kissing. I don't know. Emotions are complicated. We're just going to have to work our way through these things with love and understanding.

"What if we high-five instead?" I yell back at the child up the tree.

"Seriously?" asks Dean. "You're giving in to her?"

"Trust me."

He nods.

"That's all you're going to do?" asks Sophie suspiciously.

"We high-five here," I say. "Then go kiss for five minutes in the pantry at home, where no one can see."

"Make it ten," whispers Dean.

"Ten minutes."

The distinctly hot-and-evil smile he gives me. My panties are gone.

"No one will see?" asks Sophie.

"That's right," says Dean. "If that's what'll make you feel more comfortable today then we'll go along with it. Because we love you, and it's important that everyone in the family has a nice time."

I shake my head. "We really do need to find a therapist."

He grunts.

"I'm coming down," says Sophie.

Hands on hips, he sighs. Then he turns his gaze to me and says, "We getting married today or what?"

"Yes, we are." I cradle his face in my hands. "Took you a while, but I am finally convinced. You're prime husband material made just for me."

The edge of his mouth kicks up in a smile. "Thank fuck for that."

Continue reading for a sneak peek of

BECAUSE THE NIGHT:
A Vampire Romance

CHAPTER ONE

The house is protected by a tall, stone fence and hidden by an overgrown garden. Given the way the hinges of the wrought-iron gate screech when I push it open, I doubt anyone has been here in years. Which is weird. This Spanish Revival in the Hollywood Hills must be worth a fortune. A weed-infested gravel path leads to the large, arched, wooden front door. Three stories of white walls and terracotta roof tiles tower above me.

My boss, Jen, said to go through the place from top to bottom and make a note of anything that needed to be fixed. Any water leaks or signs of animals, etcetera. The Thorn Group doesn't normally provide this service. Guess the client is special.

Inside the house, the air is stale, and sheets cover much of the furniture. The place feels like a museum. It has all of the original features, wooden rafters on the high ceiling and French doors opening onto a courtyard. But the overall atmosphere is oppressive as fuck. When I sneeze from the dust, the sound echoes through the empty house. Same goes for my footsteps. The electricity works, but half of the bulbs are blown, and the other half are too dim to be useful. It all adds to the haunted house vibe.

I wander through room after room, carrying the set of heavy, old house keys, peering into corners and under shrouded chairs and tables. There's no security system, and yet the place hasn't been touched. It's nothing less than a miracle. A grand piano and a wall full of leather- and clothbound books take pride of place in the living room. Art and photos and antique mirrors hang on the walls. And a bar cart stocked with half-empty bottles of liquor sits beside the ornate fireplace full of ash. It looks like the owner just up and left—walked out mid-cocktail party or something.

The view is spectacular on the third-level balcony. All of the glamor and grime of the Sunset Strip. Streetlights flicker down below as the sun sinks in the west. There's an old saying about a red sunset. Some warning of the weather and things to come, but I can't remember what it is. A cold autumn breeze has me wrapping my cardigan tighter around me. Time to get this job done. There's a hot bath and a good book waiting for me at home. Though there's no food, so a grocery stop will be required. A salad from Trader Joe's sounds good, so does their sea salt brownie bites, because balance.

Taking notes on my cell, I move from room to room as night sets in. The house is in good condition for its age. And if I focus on my work, I can ignore its general spookiness—right up until a branch scrapes against a window, making me shriek.

Shit.

I rub the heel of my palm against my rib cage. My heart is hammering inside my chest. Jen not giving me urgent, last-minute jobs would be great. Exploring abandoned buildings with bad lighting is also officially not my thing. Something I might want to add to my contract moving forward. None of this situation should have happened. I entered Jen's office to ask for a raise, only to have her forget I scheduled the meeting and send me here.

Having walked through the upper, main, and lower levels (the latter of which is partially set into the hill), only the basement remains. Another of those weak lightbulbs barely illuminates the staircase. I have to force my feet to keep taking the next step and go down there.

The basement is about what I expected: a boiler and storage in one vast room. But the sheer amount of stuff down here is awe inspiring. Furniture and paintings and wooden chests. Endless racks of dusty old bottles of wine. It's like an antique store and a vineyard had a baby and that child chose chaos.

This is wild. Who owns all of this? How many generations did it take to collect it all?

I plod along, leaving footsteps in the dust. With the way the hairs on the back of my neck are standing at attention, it feels as if someone is watching me. Which is ridiculous. But then, I always did have an overactive imagination. If this were one of my true-crime podcasts, the psycho killer would absolutely be about to jump out and grab me. And each and every member of the audience would shake their heads and say what an idiot I was to enter the creepy basement. They would absolutely be right.

In the shadowy back corner is a locked door. It's made out of thick, scarred wood, as if the surface had been burnt and attacked over time. I don't want to know what's behind it. I don't even want to go near it. But I pull up my big girl panties and search the old ring of ornate keys for a match. As much as I try

to be quiet, the keys clink and scrape. Not that it matters—
there's no one here but me. I remind myself of this fact over
and over again. However, my shoulders rise higher and higher
with each passing moment.

There are six keys. I try them all, testing them against the
rock-solid lock. Until finally I am left with only one. Every fiber
of my being is praying that it won't work. Meaning my job here
is done and I can haul ass back home.

Click.

But no. The key turns and the sound of the lock releasing
echoes around the room. I've heard screams that were quieter.
My throat is so damn tight it's hard to breathe.

Nope. I can't do it. Jen can fire me for all I care. No way
am I turning the handle and opening the door to see what's inside. I've never been a big believer in the unknown. But the bad
vibes or whatever the hell they are rolling off of this door are
too intense to be denied. I don't want to know what's back there.
What I do know that I'm doing is getting out of here. Right now.

Having made the decision, my sense of relief is mighty.

A calm and reasonable person would take their time in the
low lighting. Be careful not to trip over anything. But each step
I take away from that door is faster than the last. The urge to
vacate this place is now the only thing I am feeling.

As I near the staircase, a low, menacing growl comes from
somewhere behind me. Next comes slow, shuffling footsteps.

This cannot be fucking happening. My thick thighs rub together beneath my skirt as I bolt for the staircase. Blood pounds
a hectic beat behind my ears. Forget locking the house. I just flee.
Up the stairs and out the door and through the garden and onto
the street. And my car is right there—it's all going to be okay.

But two strong arms, like bands of steel, wrap around me from behind. There's a stinging pain in the side of my neck. Some deep, animal instinct tells me it's sharp, predatory teeth stabbing through my skin. I struggle and writhe; however, there's nothing I can do. My scream echoes down the empty street and into the uncaring night. No one is coming to save me.

The attack goes on and on, draining me of my strength, robbing me of my life. It doesn't hurt exactly, at least after the first sharp sting, but it sure as hell isn't pleasant feeling my life's blood drain away.

Dark spots float before my eyes as my heartbeat slows to next to nothing. I feel myself being lowered to the ground. The asphalt is cold and rough against my back, and yet my mind is peaceful. Is this what dying feels like?

A cool hand grabs hold of my chin and a disinterested blue gaze in a gaunt face looks me over. His lean features seem to be filling out before my eyes. A hint of color returns to his ashen skin. His teeth are white, even for California, but what's bizarre is the length and sharpness of his canines. Animals have teeth like that. And other things known for biting people and drinking blood do, too.

Things I don't want to name because they're impossible, and don't exist, and oh God.

"Everything is fine," he says, meeting my gaze.

And it's true. I should be terrified, but for some reason I'm not, and I don't understand why.

If I have to die, at least I'm doing so in the presence of beauty. Because he is breathtaking. Longish dark hair and white skin with a sharp jawline, angular cheekbones, and a high forehead. He looks like a Hollywood hero, and his suit is obviously vintage. I can tell by the wide lapels and baggy pants. It's as if he just stepped out of an old black-and-white movie. Something with James Dean or Jimmy Stewart, like my grandmother used to watch when I was a child.

For a long moment, he looks up. No idea if he's staring at the streetlight, the jet plane passing overhead, or even the blinking light from a satellite high in the night sky. But his gaze is thoughtful when he turns back to me. He looks over my face and figure with renewed interest.

"I don't know this world," he says, as if to himself. Then he strokes my cheek with the pad of his thumb, before winding a lock of my hair around his finger. "And you remind me of someone. What's your name?"

"Skye."

"Skye," he repeats in a pleasant tone. "You're going to be a good girl for me, aren't you, Skye?"

Of course, I am. I would do *anything* to please him. But when I try to nod, or to speak again, nothing happens. I simply lack the strength. My whole body feels light, insubstantial. Like I might float away on the next breeze. It's then that I realize I haven't even done anything interesting with my life, and here I am, about to lose it.

With a sigh, he brings his wrist to his mouth and bites. Then he presses the wound to my lips and says, "Drink."

Blood trickles into my mouth, the scent of copper and taste of iron is overwhelming. I barely manage to swallow, but I do because I wouldn't dare disobey him. A sharp sensation spreads through me, forcing its way into my flesh and bones. It is fire without heat, and it brutally consumes me.

When I try to turn my head, he forces me back, making me

take more. I want to cry and scream and puke all at the same time. The blood flows down my throat and through my body and all I can do is lie there and…

"I know you're awake," says a deep, amused voice. "It's time we had a little talk."

I open my eyes a sliver. Just enough to see the linen bedsheet beneath my cheek and the shadows thrown by the thick candle burning on an antique wooden desk. I doubt this is Heaven. Not that I've ever been particularly religious. But when I imagined an afterlife, I pictured an eternal, peaceful darkness. A whole lot of nothing with all of my anxiety gone for good. A big old four-poster bed with a beautiful bastard sitting on a wingback chair in the corner watching me—not so much.

Though he could be the Devil. His presence is commanding as he sucks all of the air from the room. He radiates power and strength and I have never experienced anything like it. He has big dick energy to the nth.

"You attacked me. You fucking bit me." The strange thing is, I feel amazing. The best I have ever felt. Which makes no sense, and means I'm nowhere near as afraid of him as I should be. Confusion and righteous anger are my main emotions right now. "How long was I out?"

"Ladies don't swear."

"Ladies do what they like, and I happen to like salty language…a lot. Now answer the question."

"Not long." He holds up my cell. "What's this?"

"My phone."

His dark brows rise. "This is a telephone?"

"Yes. How do you not know that? Where am I?"

"In one of the basement rooms you were so clumsily try-ing to enter. It's little wonder you woke me," he says. "What year is it?"

I sit up and wrinkle my nose. "What year is it? Who are you, Sleeping Beauty?"

"Just answer the question." I tell him, and his response is, "Huh."

Something is definitely going on with me. My sight is somehow so much better. Even with only the low light of the solitary candle, I can see everything. From a couple of dust motes dancing in the air to the missed stitch on the collar of his button-down shirt. It's like looking through a magnifying glass. Seeing the world in such detail is overwhelming.

"Relax your eyes," he says. "Broaden your focus. It takes some getting used to."

"What did you do to me?"

"Have the old tales already been forgotten?"

Not only has my sight changed, but I can hear more things, too. An insect scuttling across the floor upstairs and a night bird calling in the garden. We're underground in a basement room with solid stone walls and no windows. There's no way I should know that a car is cruising past the other end of the street, or that a neighbor is playing "Saturn" by SZA.

My fingers tighten on the thick, woolen blanket thrown over the end of the bed, and the material tears as if it were wet paper. It's all too much. Scents, sights, sounds, touch, and taste. Everything has suddenly been amped up to eleven.

The asshole sighs. "You're going to break a lot of shit before you get yourself under control, aren't you?"

"What did you do to me?"

"You know." He smirks and rises to his feet. "I can see it in your eyes."

I don't know, but I do have my suspicions, as wild as they are. I run my tongue over my teeth and taste blood after one of my enhanced canines scratches it. "This is…vampires aren't real."

"If you say so," he says.

"It's not possible."

"Okay."

His amused gaze makes me want to scream. "I hate you."

"And now you have all the time in the world to do so. Isn't that nice?"

"Oh my God. You're serious."

"As the dead," he confirms.

"No. I won't kill people."

"You don't have to. Though, it takes practice to resist the urge to feed until you're satiated once the blood fills your senses." He snaps his fingers at me like I'm a dog. Asshole. "Enough of this. We have errands to run, and you'll be getting hungry soon. Come here, Skye."

There's an answering tug inside me at his words. An urge to do what he said. It's like an invisible, psychic thread linking us together.

"Look at me," he orders, gazing into my eyes. "Come here, Skye."

Once more, I feel the tug in the center of my chest. But, honestly, he can go to Hell. "I am not one of the undead, the whole idea is ridiculous. Because vampires wouldn't have panic attacks, and I'm clearly having one now. My life. My friends and family and job and—"

"Come here now." He doesn't raise his voice, but I have to cover my ears to protect them against the wall of sound that hits me. It echoes around inside my skull, all sharp edges. The agony of it is still echoing inside me as I climb off the bed. Not doing as he asks has consequences, apparently.

"That hurt," I whisper, massaging my temples. "Please don't do it again."

"So the sire bond does work on you, it just takes extra will on my part. That's going to be annoying."

"Sire bond?"

"I made you. Therefore, I'm your sire." He pushes his thick, dark hair back from his face and stares down at me. I am average height, but barely reach his broad shoulder. "Your old life is over. The best way to keep your friends and family safe is to stay away from them."

My go-fuck-yourself gaze says it all.

"You're more difficult to kill now, but it's not impossible." He circles me like a shark before taking hold of my ponytail and wrapping it tightly around his fist. Then he tugs, pulling me back against his hard body. "And make no mistake, I will end you if you don't start being useful and stop misbehaving. Do you understand?"

"Yes."

"Good." He releases me with a warning look. "Who sent you here tonight? How did you get the house keys?"

"My boss gave them to me."

"And who is your boss?"

"Are you going to hurt them if I tell you?"

He thinks it over for a second. "It's highly doubtful. I'd be more concerned about my own skin if I were you. Now…don't make me ask again."

"Jennifer Manning," I say reluctantly. "I work for a company called The Thorn Group."

He smiles. "The Thorn Group? Is that so?"

I glare at him.

Not that he cares. "Let's start there then. We have a lot of ground to cover before dawn."

To continue reading, find links to purchase below:

PURCHASE KYLIE SCOTT'S OTHER BOOKS

So My Ex Boyfriend is a Serial Killer

Because the Night

Text Appeal

The Last Days of Lilah Goodluck

End of Story
Beginning of the End (Prequel Novella)

Famous in a Small Town

THE WEST HOLLYWOOD SERIES
Fake

Love Under Quarantine

The Rich Boy

Lies

THE LARSEN BROTHERS SERIES
Repeat
Pause

It Seemed Like a Good Idea at the Time

Trust

THE DIVE BAR SERIES
Dirty
Twist
Chaser

THE STAGE DIVE SERIES
Lick
Play
Lead
Deep
Strong: A Stage Dive Novella

THE FLESH SERIES
Flesh
Skin
Flesh Series Novellas

Heart's a Mess

Colonist's Wife

ABOUT KYLIE SCOTT

Kylie is a *New York Times*, *Wall Street Journal*, and *USA Today* best-selling, Audie Award winning author. She has sold over 2,000,000 books and was voted Australian Romance Writer of the year four times by the Australian Romance Reader's Association. Her books have been translated into sixteen different languages. She is based in Queensland, Australia; living and working on land traditionally owned by the Jagera people.

www.kyliescott.com
Facebook: www.facebook.com/kyliescottwriter
Instagram: www.instagram.com/kylie_scott_books
Pinterest: www.pinterest.com/kyliescottbooks
BookBub: www.bookbub.com/authors/kylie-scott

To learn about exclusive content, my upcoming releases and giveaways, join my newsletter here: